C000275030

The Highland Heir

The Highland Heir

Allison B. Hanson

This book is a work of fiction. Names, characters, places, and incidents are the product of the author's imagination or are used fictitiously. Any resemblance to actual events, locales, or persons, living or dead, is coincidental.

Copyright 2023 by Allison B. Hanson. All rights reserved, including the right to reproduce, distribute, or transmit in any form or by any means.

Edited by Jenny Quinlan at Historical Editorial

Cover by Sarah Waites

First Edition October 2023

Chapter One

July 1546, The Scottish Highlands

If given a choice between sitting in the hall hearing auld Innes accuse his neighbor of switching out his cow with one that gave less milk or jumping from the seawall to drown in the ocean, Kieran Sinclair might have chosen the latter. But Kieran had not been given many choices in his twenty years.

The son of a laird was first and foremost *the heir*. Upon his birth, he was destined to one day take over the clan, and as such, he spent every day until that happened in constant preparation for the event.

Even if it was never supposed to be his birthright.

In truth, Kieran was to be the second son. Heir to the

heir only. Had things transpired as they should have, Kieran would be free to do what he wanted—or to do nothing at all.

Without the mantle of responsibility weighing heavy on his shoulders, he could have lived a life of his choosing, marrying his heart's desire. Not that he was interested in marrying and had no heartfelt desires of yet.

Still, he knew one day he would marry a woman that was chosen for him. He would enter into a marriage for the sole purpose of an alliance or in a trade with some other clan.

If only his older brother had lived, it would have been Brody whose destiny was written without his control.

But that wasn't how it had happened.

"I swear to ye, laird," Innes said. "The cow I had before had a spot on its leg in the exact place where Archie's cow has a mark. It proves it's my cow."

"Ye are daft," Archibald Sinclair retorted. "How would our cows have gotten mixed up? My cow has been in the shelter all day."

"Well, I know it didn't happen today, for ye switched them out last night while I was abed. Ye didn't think I'd notice this cow only gave half a pail of milk when my cow gave more than half."

Kieran looked over at his father to see if the man was in as much danger of rolling his eyes as Kieran, but, of course, that wasn't the case.

Rolfe Sinclair took everything seriously. In fact, Kieran couldn't say he remembered ever seeing his father so much as smile, let alone laugh.

Kieran had heard the stories of how happy the laird had been once, long ago, when he'd been married to his beloved Muriel and his son, Brody, had been perched on the laird's knee. The pride of his father's heart.

But Muriel had taken a fever and died when the child was only two summers, and when the lad was four, a wicked serpent of a woman had allowed the child to be claimed by the sea.

That wicket serpent had been Kieran's mother. A woman he hadn't known because she'd fallen to her death from the battlements when Kieran had been only a babe. Or at least that was one telling of it. Some said the laird had killed Kieran's mother for what she'd done to his first child.

Being born of the woman who had tricked Rolfe into marriage, Kieran also had the misfortune of looking like her, with his raven hair and green eyes. Kieran assumed it was the reason he'd never been able to earn the laird's love or respect. No matter how much he'd tried.

"Laird, I assure ye, I've done no such thing. I was in my bed last night, not out swapping cattle about."

Rolfe raised his hand, and that simple gesture brought silence to the squabbling in the hall.

"I ask ye, Innes, how would Archie know your cow gave more milk than his when the difference is not so great? Why would a man switch a cow that gives any milk with the chance of getting a cow that gave little or no milk?" The laird's icy blue gaze settled on Innes. Kieran was comforted to know it wasn't only him that squirmed under that weight.

"Well, I'm not so sure, laird."

"Cattle are rather predictable beasts. Does your cow come to your home to be milked, or has she tried to go to Archibald's?"

Innes frowned as he rubbed his chin. "Aye, she comes to mine."

"Then I think it's safe to say ye have the right cow after all. My ruling is that each of ye keep the cows ye have and I'll hear nothing more on it."

"Aye, my laird," Innes agreed.

"Thank ye, laird." Archibald seemed relieved he wouldn't have to give up his slightly better cow.

The men bowed and left in silence. No one would dare question the situation further after the laird had given his ruling.

"How would you have ruled?" Rolfe asked Kieran, as he often did.

After years of trying to impress his father, Kieran occasionally changed course and chose to purposefully irritate the man instead. It was easier to endure his father's disappointment when Kieran hadn't tried for anything more.

"I would have told them they each had a cow that gave them milk and they should be grateful for it. Then I would have told them to go away so as not to spend my life listening to petty arguments from the old codgers."

As expected, Rolfe frowned.

"If a laird doesn't listen to his people on their simpler complaints, they won't feel confident to come to him with their larger concerns. A laird who doesn't hear his people doesn't *know* his people."

"Yes, father," Kieran said because it was true, and also because it would end the lecture all the quicker for agreeing.

Before Rolfe could offer complaint for Kieran's easy acquiescence, Teague entered the hall. The war chief gave a formal nod before turning to the men following him.

"My laird, your guest has arrived. Laird MacKenzie."

"Neil," Rolfe said and stood to greet the other man, whom Kieran had never met. The other men with the MacKenzie laird must have been retainers, for they were not introduced or noticed.

Dara, the chatelaine, who seemed to know all that went on in the keep, came forward at once.

"I will have food and drink brought right away." She bustled off toward the kitchens, and Kieran wished he could escape with her.

When he'd been a lad, he'd spent much of his time in the kitchens with the women and his best friend. But now, he was expected to sit at the high table and take part in clan business.

Not that he had any idea what kind of business had brought the MacKenzie laird to their lands. His father told him little.

"How is your family?" Rolfe asked, making it sound as if he cared.

"Well, thank ye." Neil glanced at Kieran and gave a nod. "Your son looks hearty."

Hearty? Was that the word used to describe a man who stood at least four inches over his father's tall frame and was wider in the shoulder than the laird as well? Kieran might have sniffed in offense except he knew how much the sound bothered his father, and he didn't want to be scolded like a lad in front of the MacKenzie.

"Aye. He will make a fine husband to your Isla. Shall we sign the contract and then celebrate with a dram?" Rolfe suggested.

Perhaps Kieran wasn't as hearty as he'd thought, for he felt the world had just tilted as the words echoed about in his mind. Kieran would make a fine *husband*? A husband to this man's daughter?

"Marriage?" The word escaped Kieran's dry throat.

Rolfe lifted a brow and frowned at Kieran.

"Why do you look so surprised?" his father asked.

Kieran might have answered if he thought he could get the words out. The truth was he looked surprised because he was, in fact, quite surprised. Why did his father act as if it were something they'd just discussed earlier in the day?

It surely wasn't as if Kieran would have forgotten such a thing as being shackled to a wife he didn't know.

"You've known for as long as you can recall that, as my heir, you would one day be joined in an advantageous marriage when an alliance was required."

Yes. *One day.* He didn't realize it would be so soon and with a complete stranger.

Rolfe went on, nodding toward the other man as if the man came to visit often, despite Kieran never having seen him in his life. "Neil is in need of cattle. In exchange, they will guard our lower borders. And to keep everyone honest, we will join our clans in marriage."

"Aye, father," Kieran finally managed. If he had an argument, he surely couldn't think of it now. And there would be no sense in bringing it up in front of the others and putting his father on the defense. Nothing would come of arguing.

Kieran had never done anything to please his father;

he'd certainly make a mess of this as well.

As soon as he was able, Kieran left the men to their plans. Plans for Kieran's future he obviously had no say in. With his fingers clenched, he carried his anger out of the hall toward the kitchens. There was only one person he could talk to. One person who, while they couldn't understand, would at least attempt to.

Everyone looked up when he entered, perhaps because in his haste the door had banged against the wall, alerting the women inside of his presence.

He searched each face until he came to the person he was looking for. Just seeing her made his fingers relax. Her happy smile and warm brown eyes eased him as no other could.

"Ellie, I need your help."

Chapter Two

Ellisay Ross jumped along with the other women when the door to the kitchen slammed against the wall. Kieran stood there, taking up most of the opening, his face white and his light green eyes wide.

"What has happened?" Marnie, the cook, asked.

"Is it a siege?" Joan worried.

"Nay." Kieran raised one of his large hands to set them at ease. "Everything is fine. I just need to speak to Ellie, if ye can spare her a minute or two."

Ella wasn't worried there was a raid, but she knew his claim that everything was fine was not true. Something was wrong with her best friend. Kieran was beyond upset.

Being friends since they were old enough to walk

meant she knew him better than anyone, and right then she could tell he was as frantic as a wounded animal.

Wiping her hands on her apron, she hurried away and followed him outside, where he leaned over, pulling in deep breaths of warm July air.

If Ella was forced to guess, she'd say this had to do with the laird. For only the laird could upset Kieran in this manner. The laird never found an end to the list of grievances he held against his son for doing nothing more than existing.

Rolfe Sinclair was a fair laird to his clan, but didn't often extend that same courtesy to his second-born son.

Kieran was too old to cry as he had when they'd been younger, but she could tell it was serious all the same.

"What has happened?" she asked, reaching out to rest her hand on the hard muscle of his shoulder.

He remained in his position, bent at the waist with his hands braced on his knees, breathing as if he'd just run a great distance.

"I'm to be married," he managed while heaving in gusts of air.

She gasped and gripped his shoulder harder.

"How soon?" she asked.

Kieran shrugged. "I'm not sure. Why should he tell me? I'm only the groom. They're in his study signing the betrothal agreement right now."

"So soon?" She shook her head, knowing as she'd said it that it was not so soon. Kieran was twenty summers. His father could have married him off as early as ten and four.

"Aye. I shouldn't be surprised. I've known my fate for many years. I just thought there would be more time. And I thought I would at least meet the lass I was to marry."

Ella nodded. "Who is she?"

"The Mackenzie's daughter."

Ella nodded again, though she'd never set her gaze on the Mackenzie laird or his daughter. She didn't know if this was good news or not. But she knew why Kieran would be upset.

To marry a complete stranger would be unsettling to say the least. For Kieran—someone who had been torn down constantly by a father who could barely stand to look at him, let alone care for him as a father should—he was uneasy with strangers.

And now he would be taking one to wife.

"It might not be so bad. She might be beautiful. She could be witty and smart, and mayhap the three of us will be great friends," she said, trying to sound encouraging.

Over the many years they had been friends, she'd spent a great deal of time encouraging Kieran so he'd not believe the cruel things his father said.

Her hand rubbed a circle on his back as she did

whenever he was upset. She briefly wondered why she'd never noticed the way the muscles in his back pulled and twisted. The strength shifting under his skin was not unlike that of a horse.

She pulled her hand back when it felt as if the heat from his skin might burn her.

"What does my father always say?" she asked. "We get to choose to make the best of every situation." She did her best to force a pleasant tone while she squeezed and released her fingers to relieve the tingling heat that remained from touching him. She'd never suffered such an affliction before.

"Except I have no choices, Ellie. None. I can only do what my father orders me to do. Though at times I do wonder if it matters. Would he hate me any less for doing his bidding than if I resisted?"

She let out a breath. When Kieran spoke in this manner, he often got himself into trouble by lashing out against his father. Not that his father would deign to exert the effort to punish Kieran. He was simply dismissed with that casual look of disappointment from Rolfe that made Ella's blood boil.

"You know it's not your fault. When Rolfe looks at you, he can only see your mother and the pain she caused him. It's not fair, but you have to know you are a good son. Despite how he treats you."

As she watched, he seemed to calm a little more and eventually stood.

Ella didn't remember Anna Sinclair any more than Kieran did, for they were both babes when Kieran's mother died. Or was killed, depending upon what story one chose to believe.

Ella's own mother died when she was born, so she and Kieran were both raised by their fathers. But Ella's father had extended his duty to help raise Kieran as well, filling in the gaps left by the laird. Mostly in matters of affection.

Even as war chief of the Sinclair clan, Teague Ross was a sweet father and a kind man.

"And they didn't even tell you when the wedding would take place?" she asked again. Not that she wanted her friend to worry any more than he already was, but Ella wanted to know. Though she wasn't so sure why it mattered.

"Nay, though I heard the MacKenzie retainers talking. It sounds as if it will take place after harvest. The MacKenzies plan to take half the cattle with them now. The laird will bring his daughter to Girnigoe after harvest, and when he leaves, he'll take the remaining cattle for his loss."

Ella felt a flare of irritation at the way women were traded like livestock. In this case, it was even more true. She shook her head.

"I know you are upset, but can you imagine what she

must feel? To have to move to a new clan? To be exchanged for cattle?"

Ella's father had been the third son to the Ross laird, and as such, Ella didn't hold any status to speak of. It meant she wouldn't have to face such a fate as being married for the purpose of an alliance. She had the luxury of being able to marry for love.

But at almost twenty years, she had not met anyone she cared for more than Kieran. Theirs was the love of friendship, rather than what one would feel for a husband, but it had been a gauge she'd come to hold all other men to.

As of yet, no other man had been interested enough to get to know her.

She knew some thought her too rough for all the time she spent with a practice sword, sparring with her father's men.

She'd heard only a few rumors that some thought Kieran used her in his bed and therefore Ella was unsuitable for marriage. It wasn't true, and she didn't worry over what others said.

The right man would not believe such things. He would get to know her and the truth. The rest of the lot could go to the devil.

And, of course, her use of profanity, both mental and verbal, didn't help her attract potential husbands either.

"Who are you sending to the devil in your thoughts?" Kieran asked with a half-grin.

"How did you guess?"

"You're making that face." He pointed at her.

It was sometimes difficult to hide things from one's best friend.

"To be honest, I was cursing every man but you and my da."

Kieran nodded. "I'm pleased you still afford me pardon from hell."

"Always," she promised.

Kieran blew out a breath and seemed to relax. She'd seen him do the same many times as he resolved to face his fate.

"Everything will be all right," she offered another promise. But unlike the first, she didn't know if it was true.

She wanted nothing more than to make him feel better, even if she was unsure. How would everything be all right if his new wife forbid him from spending time with Ella?

What woman would allow her husband to have a woman as a best friend?

Ella would have to make it clear to Kieran's wife that she posed no threat. It should be easy enough. Other than the gossips who thought they shared a bed, most of the castle and village discounted her as a romantic interest for the laird's son.

It was almost insulting how most people never questioned their familiarity.

But now was not the time for her irritation. Kieran needed her.

"Let us go away from here," she said. He didn't need to ask where they would go. They both knew. It was the place they always went when they needed to think through a problem.

She remembered the times when one or both of them had been facing a punishment for something they'd done and they'd gather up their strength before seeing it through.

This was similar.

He was rightfully worried about what would happen to him and what his future held. It wasn't the time for her to tell him how worried she was that she might lose her best friend with the laird's decree.

But that didn't keep her from worrying.

Chapter Three

At Ellie's suggestion, Kieran followed her to the stony beach that welcomed the constant touch of the North Sea. The Sinclair lands were at the most northern tip of Scotland, and many days as a lad, Kieran had looked out over the gray waves, imagining what it would have been like to see the Viking ships come to ground before their warriors disembarked to claim or kill everything in their path.

It was that Viking heritage that Kieran saw when he looked into his father's icy blue eyes and watched his white-blond hair whipping in the wind.

Picking up another handful of smooth stones, he tossed one into the waves, losing sight of it. Throughout their lives, he and Ellie must have thrown thousands of pebbles into the surf while talking and planning.

Sometimes, like now, they were just silent. Both knowing the other would be ready to talk when it was time.

While Kieran was inside the castle, he felt as if he was bound by leather straps in an attempt to fit into the space his father allowed. But out here with Ellie, he was free to be himself. He could say anything, no matter how silly or selfish, and she would listen without judgment. He may not always like or agree with her response, but he knew it came from a place of kinship he had with no other person.

When his hand was empty of rocks, he glanced down at the scar across his palm. It was a reminder of one of many of their foolish childhood ideas.

Ellie had told him their friendship would last forever for making a blood pact. Not wanting to risk losing her, he'd eagerly agreed to let her cut him.

"Do ye ever think we could already be married?" He held up his hand.

She winced and looked down at her own palm, where a much smaller scar remained.

"The words were similar to the marriage bond, if I remember correctly," he explained.

"I may have gotten the idea from watching James and Marnie exchanging their vows when they thought they were in private."

She scrunched up her freckled nose. Her long brown hair swished across her small shoulders as she shook her head and continued.

"But nay. It can't be a real marriage unless both people consent to it. And I'm sure there must be some rules about our ages. We were only nine summers."

"All I know is you cut me up good." He held up his hand to show her the scar, causing her to frown again.

"My da never had a reason to give me a lashing before that day. When we showed up at the cottage with your hand nearly severed from your body, I thought he was going to swoon."

It was an exaggeration, but there had been a terrible amount of blood. Kieran had thought he might die.

"You didn't make the same mistake on your own hand."

Kieran sniffed and picked up a few more stones.

"'Tis lucky for us both you didn't lose the use of your hand. I would have gotten more than the switch if I'd maimed the laird's heir."

They'd both been warned many times that they couldn't afford to be careless. The fate of the Sinclair clan fell heavily on Kieran's shoulders as the only living heir.

How many times had he made the mistake of thinking his father cared about him? That he'd been worried he would lose his only living son. But it was only for being the heir that his father was concerned.

"I'm a man grown. I guess it's time I stop sniveling about my father's contempt and marry. Perhaps I'll be blessed with a son of my own. If I would be so lucky, I promise ye, I'll do things differently."

"I fear your child with be spoiled rotten for all the affection you have bottled up ready to unleash upon the poor bairn."

Kieran smiled at her wide grin.

Since he'd become a man, he'd recognized Ellie as his opposite. A woman. It was impossible not to when their bodies had changed so drastically.

When once they'd been so similar, two odd forms had evolved. Her with breasts that captured his attention at the most inopportune moments. And he continued to grow and grow until he towered over her.

"Do you remember when you used to be taller than me?" he asked her as she brushed a stray lock of brown hair back from her pretty face. Only out here in the sun could one see the threads of auburn hiding amongst the sable waves.

She rolled her brown eyes as she usually did when he got to reminiscing.

"For all of three days, maybe."

It had been longer than that. He'd been worried she

would always be taller, but that hadn't come to be. Once he started growing, it seemed he would never stop. It felt as if he grew since he'd left the castle in the morning and when he returned.

"What if my new wife doesn't wish us to be friends any longer?" He blurted out the worry he'd been trying to keep silent.

It seemed strange to be fixated on such a thing when he faced marriage to a person he'd never met as well as all the things that came with being a husband. But since those other things seemed too large to tackle at the moment, he grasped on to this worry particularly.

She seemed to freeze in the act of tossing a stone. The pebble landed just a few feet from her.

"I never thought of such a thing," she said, but he knew she was lying as only he would be able to tell. "That is, I did think of it, but *we* know we are friends and nothing more; most people don't even blink an eye in doubt. I forget that someone else—your wife—might question it."

Several years ago, one of the hired retainers had said something to Kieran about Ellie. He'd assumed she warmed his bed. He and Ellie had brushed it off as most people seemed to know better.

And the truth was that, other than one awkward kiss when they were twelve, they'd never been physical.

That kiss had been experimental for both of them. They had known they would be called upon to kiss someone at some point and decided to try it out with someone who could provide details for the betterment of the act.

The women he'd kissed since had no complaints. As for Ellie, he didn't think she'd yet had the opportunity to test her knowledge with anyone but him.

He felt a rush of guilt at this thought. He knew men avoided his friend for a number of silly reasons, but one of those reasons was him. Anyone who dared to hurt her would face the end of his sword. As if Kieran wasn't a daunting enough discouragement, her father was the war chief.

"I'll make sure this Isla knows the truth of it," he said. "And if she does take issue with our friendship, that is just something she'll have to get over. I'll not change who I choose to spend time with because of a wife."

Ellie laughed. "I have it on good authority from the women in the kitchens that many married men like others to think they are the head of their household, but, in truth, the wives are the neck that allows the head to turn."

Kieran could believe it. The women in the kitchens were formidable. He couldn't imagine any of them taking orders from a husband.

"I'll not give my wife any reason to distrust me. Therefore, when I tell her we are friends, she'll not take issue."

Ellie nodded, but it lacked the assurance he was hoping for.

"We are no longer children, Kier. Perhaps it is time for us to stop tossing rocks to the sea and make our lives into what we wish them to be."

He stood there, a few pebbles left in his hand. He knew she was right. While it made him feel more at ease, standing on the beach tossing stones did nothing to help him now.

He was a man. It was past time for him to face things as such.

He suddenly felt that he and Ellie had been wasting time these last few years. They should have been better prepared for this next stage of becoming adults.

He didn't even know what Ellie wanted. He could see now how they'd avoided certain discussions they weren't ready for. But the time had come.

"And what do you wish of your life?" he asked her. For all the years they'd been friends and all the long discussions they'd had, where he'd told her how he'd wanted to be a captain or a crofter or even a laird, he couldn't recall Ellie sharing any of her dreams with him.

She shrugged.

"I would like a husband and children. Same as any other lass."

His eyes widened. "You've never said so."

"You've never asked."

He blinked and stared at the woman hopping from rock to rock, and tried to see her with a man at her side and children clinging to her skirts.

The vision brought a stinging sensation to the back of his throat. Of course, he wanted only happiness for his beloved friend. Which made it more difficult to explain his intense reaction to her desires.

He didn't like it. Not one bit.

*

Ella carried another full pitcher of ale out to the high table. She rarely served in the hall, but with their extra guests with the MacKenzies visiting, Ella had offered to help. She made a face when only Kieran was looking at her, causing him to smile as she knew it would.

He was lovely when he smiled. The fact that he rarely smiled in the presence of others made those moments even more precious to her.

"Lass, I'm parched," the man at the end of the table said. He was with the Mackenzies, but from his placement at the table he was not related to the laird. A retainer most likely.

"I believe I've filled your tankard three times already

this evening," she answered as he held it out yet again.

"Perhaps I'm drinking it all the faster so you'll come close and fill it yet again, lass."

He was a handsome man, but she'd noticed the way his gaze flicked down her body when he thought she wasn't aware. His thorough inspection had nothing to do with her as a person. He only wished to sate his desires with a serving maid and move on to the next.

She'd seen such a reaction on occasion with other men and had managed to avoid such entanglements. When she was ready to give her body to a man, it would be someone she loved and someone who loved her in return.

She'd long cast off her silly fantasies about Kieran being that man. She assumed it was normal for her to think of him like that, him being the only man she was close to who was not related to her.

But Kieran had never looked at her in such a way. And she knew they would never be allowed to marry, even if he had a mind to. He was the laird's heir after all. He would be expected to marry well.

Not the daughter of the war chief. She was respectable enough, but such a marriage wouldn't bring anything of value to the Sinclair clan. The Ross and Sinclair clans were already allied.

Odd how that thought brought a tug of disappointment

to her chest. Of course, she didn't wish for Kieran to lust after her. She'd have no choice but to kick him in the cods. But the fact that he didn't think of her as a woman, or feel any attraction to her whatsoever, was somewhat disheartening.

If he didn't find her attractive, who would?

Shaking her head, she turned to leave the man to his drink, but he reached out and snagged her arm, nearly making her drop the pitcher. Before she'd realized how she'd gotten there, she was seated in the man's lap and his face was much too close to hers.

She struggled to get out of his hold, but the movement seemed to please him more.

"That's it, keep up your wiggling. You'll be a sweet bit."

"Let me up," she demanded, pushing his face away as he came closer. But he only held her tighter.

Letting out a breath, she knew there was nothing for it. He'd given her no choice but to haul off and hit him. She'd worn her favorite kirtle this evening, and it would be a pity to have it stained with this oaf's blood.

Maybe if she hit him somewhere other than his nose, she wouldn't have to manage the river of blood such a wound caused. But the rest of the man's face would be too hard and not cause as much pain.

Clenching her fist, she prepared for the sickening

crunch and drew back to deliver a strike that would ensure her freedom. But the blade of a dirk against the man's neck wiped the predatory grin from his face.

"Let her go." Kieran's already low voice was so deep it was more rumble than anything. "Now."

The man lifted both hands, and Ella didn't waste a moment. She made a point to press her knee into the softness between his legs as she maneuvered away from him. He grunted and hissed a curse.

"I didn't know she was yours," the man said.

Ella expected Kieran to say she wasn't his. Perhaps he would even give the man a firm lecture about the treatment of women on Sinclair lands or explain how Ella belonged to no one but herself.

But instead, Kieran dropped the blade and glared at the man.

"Now ye know. Don't forget it."

He'd claimed her?

She didn't know how she felt about that. She'd expected to feel annoyed, but something else kept her from calling him out. Some warm tingling sensation in her stomach at the knowledge that she was his to protect.

It was silly. She knew Kieran had only done so because it was the easiest solution to keep the man from harassing her further.

But still, she couldn't lie to herself.

She'd liked it more than she should.

Chapter Four

That night, after she wished her father a good night and went to her bed, she was still thinking of what Kieran had said. The feeling was still there hours later as she tossed and turned. If anything, it had grown warmer and more pleasant.

Even more surprising was the way the sensation followed her eventually into sleep.

She dreamed of them as they'd been earlier in the day on the shore, tossing stones into the sea. But Kieran stood closer than he had then. And when she looked up at him, he was smiling at her in the way he always did when she'd managed to amuse him. That sweet smile that flashed his white teeth.

Such a rare thing; she felt like a queen to have earned it.

Only this time, when the smile faded, the warmth remained in his eyes. He bent down and pressed his lips to hers.

They had kissed before. An odd push of their lips together at a time they thought to explore the differences in their growing bodies. It had not been unpleasant, but it had not been like this.

He'd claimed her in the great hall to save her, but in her dreams his claiming of her mouth set her free. His warm breath caressed her face as his tongue searched for hers.

His hands trailed over her body. Each touch tingled until her skin felt alive. She reached for him, wanting to feel him against her. She knew how a man and a woman joined together.

She didn't have personal experience with such a thing, but Kieran had explained it to her. She'd thought it disgusting, but now as she throbbed in the lower part of her that would be filled by him, it wasn't disgust she felt it was—

"Ella . . . Ellisay!" What was her father doing here?

She opened her eyes to her dark room. Dark except for her father standing over her with a candle lit. She squealed in alarm.

"Ye were having a nightmare, lass."

"A nightmare?" It was no nightmare, that was for certain. She didn't know what it had been, but she surely hadn't been frightened.

"You were moaning as if ye were in pain. I thought to spare you from it."

"Ah. Well, thank you, da." She lay back as her father left, taking the light with him. She stared up into the darkness, remembering the dream and trying desperately to hold on to the feeling.

For whatever reason, it seemed important to burn each kiss, each touch, into her memory so she could recall it later. As if she would someday want to lie in bed thinking about Kieran in that way whilst he lay in his chamber in the castle with his wife.

The tingling she'd felt earlier vanished at that vision, and she felt an empty pain in her chest. The pain that came from longing for someone she could never have.

"Lord, help me," she whispered.

*

Life went on after the MacKenzie laird left with his guards and half the cattle promised. For Kieran, it was as if the man had never been there. As if Kieran wasn't promised to a woman he'd never met.

The truth would come soon enough. He had only a few months until he would be wed, and he chose to spend that time not thinking about that fate. If only Ellie would cooperate.

"Do you think she will be pretty? How do you imagine her? Fair or dark-haired?" Ellie asked.

"I try not to think of it at all," he answered as he had the last dozen times she'd asked such things. Would Isla be witty? Would she know her letters and numbers? Would she like kissing?

That last one in particular caused him grief, for he was forced to imagine such a thing as kissing this wife he didn't know. Unfortunately, without the details needed to form the vision properly, his mind filled in her features with the one woman he would never kiss. That is, he would never kiss *again*.

Ellie nodded as if appeased by his answer, despite his grumbling.

"That is probably for the best. If you don't have a picture of her in your mind, you'll be less likely to be disappointed if she doesn't look how you'd imagined."

He agreed with her reasoning, but it wasn't the reason he hadn't considered such things about his intended. Thinking about Isla tended to make him think about Ellie in a way he never had before.

Well, maybe he had thought of her in his bed, kissing her in the past, but he did his best to shut them out as quickly as they'd entered his mind in some torture brought on merely by lust.

Fortunately, she relented as they went hunting together that afternoon after he'd finished with drills and bathed in the loch. It was common for them. She was quite clever with the bow, and her smaller feet made no noise as she melted into the forest like a wood sprite.

He found himself watching her as he hadn't in some time. The curve of her elegant neck, the way her hips flared enticingly in the trews she preferred to wear while hunting. The strength in her arms as she drew back her bow and let the arrow fly. The squeal of delight and the wide smile when she found she'd hit her mark.

How would he survive without those smiles? He felt as if he needed them as much as his daily meals, but instead of his stomach, her smiles fed his soul.

When they'd finished their hunt, they headed back to the castle.

"Do you wish to carry them?" she asked, holding out the rope with the rabbits they'd caught.

He sniffed and shook his head.

"It's been quite some years since I've needed to carry the rabbits. You always get more than me, and as a man, I don't need anyone to think otherwise. I've nothing to prove."

There'd been a time when he'd allowed the men's teasing to bother him about her success in the field. A prickle of shame raced through him that he'd insisted on carrying their quarry. It seemed a silly thing now.

"I wasn't asking because I thought your pride would be hurt if I carried more than you, I simply didn't want to strain myself under my large load, and you've hardly any to carry."

He laughed at her teasing and then reached out to give her a shove. She stepped out of line but didn't stumble. Probably because she expected such a reaction from him.

"If you'd not have rubbed it in, I might have offered to carry them, but now I'll leave it to you. Maybe next time you won't try so hard to outshoot me."

He only allowed her to struggle with the larger load a few more steps before he stopped and grabbed the rabbits.

As he did so, he stepped closer than he intended. His body was touching hers. Just barely, but enough to light something in him. He breathed in deeply, and the sensation was made worse by her scent.

Sunshine, clean air, and heather. Kieran didn't think Ellie did anything to capture the scent, it seemed to cling to her from all the time she spent running wild in the Highlands as a girl.

"I don't think I thanked you for that night," Ellie said as she turned from him and started walking again.

"What night?" He pressed his memories, trying to remember what he might have done to earn her thanks.

"When the MacKenzie guard pulled me into his lap."

Kieran frowned at the memory. He'd wanted to drag the man out of the keep and draw his sword for how he'd disrespected Ellie.

"I saw you'd made a fist and were planning to take care of the matter yourself. Your way would have had a rush of blood ruining our meals."

"Not to mention my favorite dress," she explained, causing him to laugh.

He nodded. "The blue suits you."

"Compliments and carrying the load of our spoils— why, Kieran Sinclair, I do think you will make the MacKenzie lass a fine husband after all."

That thought lingered as they made their way back to the castle.

Would Kieran make a good husband?

He'd little experience with marriage. His father had never married after Kieran's mother died. Teague had never married after Ellie's mother passed. Most of the warriors he spent his days sparring with were unwed.

Marnie and Joan from the kitchens were both wed, but

they were no docile brides.

"You will be a fine husband, Kier. Stop worrying," Ellie said as if she'd heard every thought as he had it.

"Careful, witch, if the wrong person finds out ye are all-knowing, you'll be burned at the stake."

"I trust ye to keep my secret." She winked at him, and he felt his body tighten in an uncomfortable way.

"Aye. But only because I don't want to be tasked with collecting all that wood," he joked, earning a thump against his shoulder.

She laughed at his jest, and he laughed along with her. He found himself wishing for this in his marriage. This easy partnership. Friendship and understanding.

He doubted he would have such a thing with a stranger. It had taken a lifetime for he and Ellie to know each other so well they didn't need to speak aloud to know the other's thoughts.

That night when he went to bed, he lay there trying to envision what his wife might look like. Ellie had asked if he pictured her fair or dark. He allowed his mind to drift as if it would lead him to a preference of some kind.

Dark. Small flashes of auburn where the sunlight touched it.

Her hair would have the slightest waves. She wouldn't be too short or too tall. Long, strong limbs and feminine curves that his hands would fit against perfectly.

And her laugh would warm his soul.

Before he'd realized it, the woman he'd conjured up blinked her brown eyes at him as if she was just as surprised to be there as he was.

"Ellie," he whispered and closed his eyes, trying to push the vision away.

Surely, he'd only thought of her because he knew every line and curve of her face. She was familiar and comfortable. But for all of those things, she was still beautiful.

He clenched his hands into fists, wishing they weren't so empty. He'd much rather have them molded to her womanly curves.

As he considered it longer, he was shocked to realize Ellie was exactly what he would want his wife to look like. How had he never seen his best friend in that way until now?

And more importantly, how would he make sure he never thought of her like that again?

Chapter Five

Ella lay in her bed in the loft above her father's room, where she'd slept since she was able to climb the ladder to the second floor. But her familiar room didn't bring her comfort tonight.

She was restless, and her mind wouldn't still. Instead, it brought up memories from the past in no discernable order. But each thought was of Kieran.

She remembered him chasing her in the fields as they often did. When they were younger, he could never catch her. She was quick with longer legs while he was lanky but slower. But when they'd been near sixteen summers, he'd grown almost a foot and he'd caught her. They'd fallen to the grass, his long body pressed against hers, and the scent of his heated skin had made her heart beat even faster.

He'd stared at her in shock a moment later, and she'd felt something move beneath his kilt before he'd rolled off her and walked away. At the time, she'd been too young to understand what had happened. But now, as a woman, she realized what it had been. Desire.

It was the first she'd thought of it since it had happened. He'd been aroused by their closeness.

Of course, she'd also learned from the women in the kitchens that lads of that age were aroused by a warm breeze, so it was surely not because of her that he'd reacted in that way.

They had never been anything more than friends. Except that one day when they'd kissed.

They'd only been twelve, and they'd seen the stable master kissing a maid. It was a strange thing for them. For their fathers had been alone since they were young, so they'd never witnessed kissing prior to that day.

"Why do you think they put their lips together like that? He looked as if he was going to eat her face," she'd asked.

Kieran had chuckled. "She didn't seem to mind. Not with the way she said, 'More,' before she hauled him away into one of the stalls."

"Should we try it to see if it is as wonderful as they made it seem?" Ella had been the one to ask.

Kieran shook his head and looked a bit disgusted by her offer.

His rejection peaked her anger and she turned away.

"Fine, I'll go find someone else to kiss, then. Maybe Raymond will be willing to try it."

Kieran grasped her arm and she turned back to him, knowing what she would find.

"The hell you'll let that daft arse kiss ye." He took a deep breath before looking back at her. "Fine. I'll do it."

She crossed her arms and waited, but he didn't make a move to come closer.

"Do ye plan to do it today?" she pushed.

"Aye. I just need a minute."

"You look the same as ye do when Cook serves pottage. Do you think kissing me will be as bad as cabbage soup, Kieran?"

Despite her anger, he didn't back away, nor did he answer. Just when she planned to walk away to go find Raymond, Kieran made his move. He grasped her upper arms and leaned in to press his lips to hers.

At the time, she'd found it rather uneventful. He held his position for some time as if waiting for something to happen. When it clearly hadn't, he'd pulled away and looked at her.

She shrugged. "I certainly don't feel like I need more of that."

"Do you think I did it wrong?" he asked. Kieran was used to being told he did everything wrong. Even if she thought he'd done this wrong, she would never have said so. And, in truth, she didn't think he had.

He'd placed his lips against hers, moved them around a bit, and then stepped back. Just as the stable master had done with the maid. Yet Ella had not lost control of her breathing or begged for more.

"Nay. I'm sure you did it just right. Mayhap it's only for adults," she'd reasoned.

Now, lying in her bed alone, she knew she'd been right. For just the thought of that long-ago kiss had caused her breathing to escalate. She wished she'd held on to the details of the moment.

What had he tasted like? Had his lips been soft? Warm? Had he closed his eyes?

She thought of Kieran the way he was now, a man grown, and how it might feel to have him holding on to her arms firmly, but not painfully. Pulling her closer so he might press his lips to hers.

She knew now that some kisses happened with

tongues. Kieran had been the one to confirm it after he'd kissed Aggie from the village.

Ella hadn't felt jealous at the time, but now she did. If Agatha hadn't already married and had two babes, Ella might have found her and given her a right shove to the ground for kissing Kieran.

"Lord," she whispered. What had caused such a strange reaction?

Kieran was a large, strong man. She also knew he was handsome, and not only because the maids in the hall always said as much, but because Ella found him to be so as well.

She shook her head, hoping to give her brains a shaking and dislodge such bizarre thoughts so she might find her sleep.

But the more she tried to think of Kieran as her friend, the more she remembered all the times he'd been close to her and how she wished for it again.

She blamed her dream and worried if she fell asleep thinking of Kieran, she would dream of him again and disrupt her father.

After spending the night tossing and turning with hardly any sleep, she gave up and went to help Marnie in the kitchens. The cook started early in the morning, making bread and other things so the warriors could break their fast before they began training for the day.

"You're up and about early this morn," Marnie noted.

"Aye. I don't wish to speak of it."

The woman laughed. "If you didn't wish to speak of it, ye shouldn't have told me ye didn't wish to speak of it. For now, you've piqued my curiosity."

Ella could have easily come up with something else to appease the woman's interest, but as she looked around the empty room confirming they were alone, Ella decided she might want to speak of her concerns.

"Do you promise not to tell another soul?"

Her smile dropped away as she stepped closer. "This sounds quite serious. Are ye well?"

"Aye. Just . . . unsettled."

"About what?"

"Recently, I've been having dreams about someone I considered a friend. But these dreams have made me think of things I shouldn't want with . . . this person."

Marnie's eyes went wide, and a kind smile pulled at her lips.

"I was beginning to think ye weren't interested in men. Some women aren't. They prefer the company of other women. You've been close with Kieran since ye were a wee lass. I was waiting for this to happen one day."

"I didn't say it was Kieran."

She sniffed. "Didn't need to. He's a fine-looking man.

And the two of ye are quite close. It's only natural ye would grow an attraction." She frowned. "Damned inconvenient it would happen now when he's to be married."

"You canna say anything to anyone. Not even James." Her husband was one of the warriors. If he knew, he might tell the others and soon everyone would know her shame.

"I'll not say a thing, though I'm sure many assume there is some interest between ye. If not from you, then from him."

It was Ella's turn to look surprised.

"You think Kieran might feel the same way about me?"

"He is a man, and you're a pretty lass. Why wouldn't he?"

"He's never said so."

"Neither have ye."

That was true enough. But to think that Kieran might be tossing about in his bed, unsettled from dreams he had about her . . . She found she rather liked the idea and hoped it to be true.

Any excitement she felt over the thought was quickly replaced by disappointment.

"It doesn't matter if he does feel the same way. There's nothing to be done for it. He's to be wed."

Marnie shrugged and looked toward the door again

before leaning closer to whisper.

"So long as ye are careful, there'd be no breaking of vows if ye were to do it now."

"Do you mean . . . ? To lie with Kieran when we're not married?" Ella's voiced raised in surprise, and Marnie swatted and shushed her.

"It is not uncommon. My James and me had a bit of pleasure before we married. But again, one must be careful. Do ye know what I mean by that?"

Ella blinked, feeling quite overwhelmed by the entire conversation. She suddenly noticed all the sleep she'd missed the night before as exhaustion set in.

"You mean his seed?" Ella asked, feeling her cheeks go red in the same way they had when the women had spoken on the subject a few months ago. At the time, Joan had said she didn't want to get with child until her youngest was a bit older. But her husband didn't like having to pull away at the crucial moment. Whatever that was.

"Aye. Babes can still happen even if he takes care with where he spills it, but it's not as likely."

She couldn't imagine speaking to Kieran of such things. But she was curious.

*

Kieran jumped out of the way a second too late and took a blade across his stomach from Raymond. It was a good thing it was a practice sword with no sharp edge to the steel or he would have been done for.

"What's wrong? You're slow as a frozen stream today," Teague said with a glare.

Kieran couldn't tell the war chief he was tired. Not when the reason he hadn't slept well was because he was thinking of the man's daughter in a disrespectful and unsettling way.

"Forgive me," he said with a nod. "Just tired."

"Did ye and Ella get into some trouble?"

"What? Nay," Kieran was quick to answer. Though he worried he'd reacted as if attempting to cover a lie. Why did he feel so uneasy looking Teague in the eye?

Perhaps because I spent the greater part of the night thinking of his daughter in disreputable ways.

"Nay," he repeated, trying to shake off the shame.

"She hasn't been sleeping well either. She's troubled with bad dreams. I've seen her like this when she's guilty over something."

"I can't say as to what she would feel guilty about," Kieran protected for his friend. It was true he didn't know anything, but even if he did, he wouldn't have told her father.

The gash across his palm promised loyalty to each

other above all others, and any secrets they shared would never be spoken.

Teague pointed his finger at Kieran, and his brows came together in a fierce frown.

"Don't think I didn't notice the choice of your words, that ye *can't say* rather than you dinna ken. I would hope as a man grown ye would have gotten past this secrecy."

Kieran laughed and shook his head.

"'Tis true, I wouldn't tell you if I did know. But I truly don't know."

Teague made a grumpy noise and nodded to the other men.

"Get back to work, and for the love of Christ, keep watch on your side when ye raise your sword. I'll not be carrying you back to the castle after a battle. Your father would have my head on a pike."

Kieran sniffed and shook his head.

"Because he would care so much for the loss of a son he despises."

"He doesn't despise ye, Kier. He may not have much of a heart left after what he's gone through, but what pieces there are would break if he were to lose you too."

Kieran nodded, though he didn't believe any of what Teague said. Kieran had seen no evidence of even a sliver of the man's heart left.

He managed to get through the rest of drills without incident, and after the midday meal he gave Ellie a nod to let her know he was heading to the beach.

She caught up to him before he was through the castle gates. For having shorter legs, she was quick as a fairy.

He should have known there would be a reason for her to be in such a hurry today.

She waited only until they were barely into the woods before she stopped and grasped his arm to hold him as well.

"I must ask you something," she said.

"Aye." It wasn't like her to warn him first. She usually just blew him over with whatever thought was on her mind.

"Have you lain with a woman before?" she asked.

He realized no amount of warning would have prepared him for this.

Chapter Six

After Kieran managed to stop choking, he cast a glare in Ellie's direction.

"What kind of question is that to ask me? Ye shouldn't be speaking of such things. You're a maiden." He knew well their friendship gave them certain freedoms when it came to proper topics, but this?

"I know what I am," she said, only the slightest change of color in her cheeks to prove she understood this was improper. "But I'm not sure what *you* are."

"And you don't need to."

"Please, Kier. We've never had secrets between us

before."

"Aye, we have, we just didn't speak of them. Just as we won't speak about this."

He didn't want to speak of this with Ellie. And not just because it wasn't honorable to speak to a woman about such things. Actually, it wasn't because of that really at all. He was only grasping on to that as an excuse.

He and Ellie had not held themselves to such proprieties before. They'd talked about all sorts of topics that wouldn't have been proper because of her being a woman and he being a man.

But this . . . nay. He didn't want to speak of it with her.

"You haven't," she said, sounding sure of herself. He kept his expression steady. He didn't want her to know she was right.

He'd never been embarrassed to talk about many things to Ellie, but this was different.

At his age, he should have a vast knowledge and a wealth of experience, like the other men, but he didn't.

And not for lack of opportunities. When he'd been young, or rather younger than he was now, he'd had women offer themselves to him often, but after years of passing them over they eventually stopped asking.

He'd been grateful at the time, but now he rather

wished he'd have just done it so it would be over with. Any woman would expect him to know his way at this point.

He knew enough from Teague to know it was left to a man's father to see this deed done when a boy turned into a man. And Kieran had waited, but his father never talked to him on the topic.

When he'd asked Teague, the chief had told him not to get a babe on a woman who wasn't his wife. He said the laird wouldn't take kindly to find Kieran sired a bastard, let alone a number of them.

Kieran allowed Teague to think he'd taken care of the matter of his virginity when, in fact, he had not. He never felt comfortable with any woman. Not enough to do such a thing with her. He thought he should care for her at least as much as he cared for Ellie before joining with her, and he never had. Perhaps using his friendship with Ellie as a gauge had been a mistake. But it was too late to change that.

And now his shame would be shared with Ellie.

"It's not your business," he said with a sneer, hoping she'd let it drop. Of course, she didn't.

"It may not be my business, but I know you've not lain with anyone. If you had, you would have said so. You wouldn't have allowed me to keep deviling you about it. You would have put an end to it."

"Mayhap I knew if I told you, it wouldn't keep you

from deviling me over who it had been."

She tilted her head from side to side as if inspecting him like a bird did to a tasty worm. To falter or so much as glance away would be failure, so he kept his gaze on hers.

Eventually, she relented.

"I can't tell if that's true or not. But you're right. I do want to know who it was. It better not have been Aggie. She always acted as if she knew something I didn't. Please tell me it wasn't her."

"Nay. It wasn't her." Though she'd been one of the lasses to offer herself to him before she'd married.

"Then who?" Ellie pressed.

"A man doesn't talk about such things. It's disrespectful."

"Nay. It's disrespectful for a man to tell other men such a thing, for they might expect the same service for themselves. That's not the case with us, so you can tell me and know I'll never share it with another soul." She held up her scarred hand in promise.

"What if it is something I wish to keep for myself?" He placed his scarred hand over his heart. With a sigh, she relented.

"Very well, I guess that is fair. But will you tell me if she was a virgin?"

"All women were virgins at some point," he deflected.

"You know what I mean. Was she a virgin when she lay with you?"

Kieran bit his lip as he struggled to determine why she was asking this particular question, as well as how he might get out of answering. Nay, not answering, but *lying* to his best friend.

"Why do you ask?" He tilted his head, watching her for more information. The things she didn't say aloud.

"I want to know if she seemed to be in a great amount of pain and if there was a lot of blood."

Damn. He wouldn't mind to know this as well. It was yet another reason why he'd not taken such a chance before. The business of bedding a virgin seemed plagued with unpleasantries.

"I can't say," he answered without looking at her.

He saw her nod.

"I figured any of the maids who would have sought ye out for such a thing would have known their way around it already."

"Why does it matter?"

"I'm thinking I'd like to do it, but . . . I'm afraid."

He'd been wise not to take another drink until the subject had been changed. Her answer surely would have had him choking again.

Not only was he surprised to hear she wished to do

such a thing, but for Ellie to admit to being afraid of anything was a rare thing.

"You'd like to get married?" he asked after clearing his throat.

"Nay. At least I can't think of anyone I'd want to marry. But I don't want to spend my life a maiden. There's no reason why I should have to wait if I don't wish to."

"There are plenty of reasons. Firstly, you don't want to get in the family way when you're unwed. Secondly, if there's no one here you'd wish to marry, why would you think they deserved the gift of your virtue? And thirdly, I don't want to have to kill a clansman for having touched ye."

She laughed at his chivalry, but that was typical for Ellie. She always thought he was teasing her, even when sometimes, like now . . .

He was not.

*

"Men have relations when they are not wed. Why should it be different for a woman?" Kieran had never been one to treat her different because she was a lass. When they hunted together, he expected as much from her as anyone else. When they sparred together, he never held back, telling her any man she had reason to fight with a sword would not go easy on her. And whenever they spoke, he bared everything without consideration of her being a woman.

Sometimes she thought he might not even notice she was a female.

It wasn't like him to use this reasoning against her.

"I don't know *why* it should be different, but it just is."

"As a matter of mathematics, the men canna have relations with women they are not married to if the women do not also have the liberty of having relations with men they are not married to."

"Mathematics is another thing women aren't to know."

She gasped as if he'd lashed her physically. She gave him a hearty push with both hands on his chest.

Only because he was standing next to a downed log did her effort cause him to stumble and fall back on his arse. She'd not been able to topple Kieran with a shove since they were children.

Rather than help him up, she turned and stormed back to the castle.

"Ellie?" he called after her, but she kept going.

She was only a few feet into the meadow when he caught up to her. He stepped in front of her and held up a hand.

"I'm sorry. Of course, I'm glad your da taught both of us our letter and numbers. And ye helped me more than a few times to make sense of things when they seemed to scramble on the page. I shouldna have said such a thing."

"Why did ye?" she asked, crossing her arms.

"Because I knew it would make you mad, and then we wouldn't have to speak about things I *really* don't want to talk about with you."

She twisted her lips to the side and sighed.

"Then I apologize as well. Ye said you didn't want to speak on it. I should have stopped. And I shouldn't have pushed you on your arse." She couldn't help but smile at the memory of him going over though. It was like a horse being pushed over by a mouse.

"It would be easier to believe you were sorry for it if ye didn't look so amused."

Pressing her lips together, she did her best to look contrite and probably failed.

He nodded anyway, easily accepting her apology.

"I should get back," she said, wanting some time alone to think about her plan.

"Ellie?" he said, stopping her.

"Aye?"

"It shouldn't be different for ye. But please be careful. If you decide to do this . . ." He frowned and looked up at the sky as if hoping for a bird to drop the words down to him. "Make sure the man is worthy of such a beautiful gift."

For a moment, as he looked at her, she couldn't

breathe. Or swallow. Or speak. She only managed to bob her head a few times before she turned to retreat.

She didn't quite understand her reaction except to say he had never used the word *beautiful* in regards to her before. It was silly, and even now it wasn't as if he'd said she was beautiful. But it had knocked the air from her lungs and all thought from her head.

She went back to the kitchens to help with the late meal, but her head wasn't in it.

She heard the other women chatting and gossiping, but she didn't really listen. When they laughed, she looked up from where she'd been kneading a mound of dough.

"You've nearly worked that dough back to being flour," Joan said. "Is something bothering ye?"

"Nay," Ella lied. In truth, everything in her life was a mess, now including the flat bread they would have for supper. Her best friend was going to leave her behind. Even if his new wife liked Ella and wasn't threatened by their friendship, things would change.

What was worse was that she now wanted her own change but had no idea how to go about making it happen.

Everything was out of control and only got worse when she went to the hall to help serve the meal.

She watched the maids that flirted with Kieran, wondering which one of them had lain with him. No doubt her distraction was the reason she spilled a flagon of ale and then carried out a bowl with nothing in it.

Her thoughts were in a muddle after talking with Kieran about joining.

But seeing the kind disinterest he offered every woman in the hall made her more certain than ever that he'd never been with a woman, maiden or otherwise.

It was the reason she relented on her plan to ask him to help her find a man who might show her what she might otherwise never know. Someone with whom she could share her *beautiful gift*, as he'd called it.

But if Kieran was being his protective self over a nameless, faceless man, she feared what might happen if she decided on exactly who she might give her virtue to.

And that problem felt as if it were a bucket of eels, twisting back on each thought, because in the end she only wanted to give her virtue to one person. But he was to marry in a few months and only thought of Ella as a friend.

Still, since she'd thought of him in that place next to her, touching her, she could think of no other. And she wanted it. More and more each day. Worse, the wanting was turning into unrest that made her snappish with anyone who spoke to her.

"What did Alasdair say to make you slam his trencher down so hard?" Kieran asked after the morning meal was over a few days later. "If he said something rude, you'll tell me so I can deal with him appropriately."

"And what will you do to any man who flirts or makes lewd comments? Will you thrash them all? What about when you are married? Will you still see it as your duty to protect me when you have a wife to protect?"

"Alasdair made lewd comments? What exactly did he say?" Kieran asked, completely missing her point.

"Nay. He said nothing. I'm just not in a good mood today."

"Oh," he said before glancing down her body and taking a step back.

"It's not my courses, you oaf."

"Are ye sure? Sometimes you get upset well before they arrive."

This was the problem. Or at least one of the many. He knew her too well. It was impossible to keep anything from him. Even things she could never speak out loud.

"I'm sorry I ever told you about that." In fact, Ella was sorry she ever told him anything and wished they'd never been friends. For if she didn't know him so well, it might not hurt so much to know he only saw her in that way.

"I have to go."

"Where? I can help if you're doing the laundry," he offered. In truth, doing the wash was easier with him to help her because, with his strength, he was able to wring out more of the water. And she hated that too.

"Nay. It's womanly. Just go do your drills with the men."

"Ellie? Did I do something?"

She wanted to scream that yes, he had, he'd made her want him, but she couldn't. It wasn't his fault. In truth, he had not changed in how he talked with her or how he looked at her. It was she who had changed. He didn't wish to marry any more than she wanted him to, so he was not to blame for the fact that her life was turning upside down and her insides were filled with hurt and worry for her future.

Yet she wanted to shake him. And then kiss him. And then have him hold her while she cried.

Bloody hell, mayhap her courses were on the way after all.

She stormed off to her cottage. Alone. Which was how she would be the rest of her life.

Chapter Seven

Kieran was sitting in the great hall with his father the next day as the man heard complaints from the clan. But Kieran wasn't hearing anything that had been said.

He was still trying to comprehend what to do about Ellie. Had he been superstitious, he would have thought she'd been a changeling for how different she was from the friend he'd known all his life. But fairies didn't steal grown adults, only babes.

He'd left her alone the last few days, as she'd asked. He hadn't even seen her that morning in the hall serving the meal.

He missed her.

He missed the way she rolled her eyes at him when the maids flirted at his table. He missed hunting with her and their silent communication they shared in the quiet forest. He missed throwing stones along the shore and talking about anything that crossed his mind.

Maybe it was for the best to get through this now. If growing apart was inevitable after his marriage, he would end up feeling this way eventually anyway.

"My laird." Teague came to stand before the laird. The man was rarely so formal, always with a smile on his face, like his daughter. But at the moment, he looked rather pale. The war chief's distress caused a shiver of worry to go through Kieran's frame.

Where was Ellie? Was she well?

"I would ask you to give me leave to go to the Ross lands. I've received word that my older sister has fallen ill. I wish to take Ella to her. She has become a fine healer and might be able to help the woman."

Kieran relaxed to know Ella was fine. But the thought of her being away from him indefinitely bothered him. He cursed his selfishness. Of course, he didn't want any pain to fall on Ellie's aunt.

Kieran looked to his father, and even before the man spoke, Kieran knew what his answer would be.

"I can't have you away from the castle at the moment. Not when I've sent Alasdair and Raymond to Edinburgh. I'm sorry."

Teague nodded and turned without argument.

"I could escort Ellie to her aunt," Kieran spoke up. His father seemed to have forgotten he was even sitting next to him. "It wouldn't hurt to speak to the Ross laird and make his acquaintance. It's been some time since I've seen him. Not since I was a lad."

"Yes, fine," Rolfe said with a wave of his hand.

"I'll pack my things right away and meet Ellie in the bailey," he said for Teague's sake since the laird had moved on to other things. Why would the man be bothered to wish his son safe travels?

If Kieran thought his father would care about him more now that he was betrothed, he would have been wrong. His father was just as indifferent as ever. Not even looking at Kieran.

He couldn't remember the last time his father had actually looked at him with anything other than anger or disappointment on his face. It was nothing but a waste of time to wish for anything different.

Kieran was not the son the laird had wanted. He wasn't the beloved result of a love match between Rolfe Sinclair and his cherished Muriel. He wasn't Brody Sinclair.

Not for the first time, Kieran wondered what his life might have been like if Brody had lived. He often thought it would have been better to have a brother with which to confide in when he was upset by his father, but he'd had Ellie for that.

And what if his brother was more like their father, and he had *two* people who hated and resented the very sight of him? It was much easier to think about all the ways his life would have been made worse by having a brother.

But at times, he saw glimpses of how it might have been if having Brody would have kept his father's heart from drying up completely. Would the laird have enjoyed having two little boys running around? Would he have played with them both? Would he have loved them both?

Such thoughts made no difference. Kieran was a man now. And for the next few days at least, he would have a reprieve from sitting next to his father at Girnigoe and bearing his indifference.

"I'll have the horses brought round," Teague said, shaking him from his thoughts. "Thank ye for seeing Ella safely to Kildary."

As Kieran threw a few things into his bag, he realized how excited he was to be away from Girnigoe Castle and, more importantly, his father. But it wasn't until they were riding out through the gates that Kieran realized the other cause for his delight.

He was with Ellie. Alone.

It was almost insulting that no one suggested others join their party for propriety's sake at least. No one else would be needed to protect Ellie. Teague knew Kieran was a fierce warrior and would give his last drop of blood in defense of the chief's daughter. But didn't anyone care about Ellie's reputation?

It was not even questioned that an unmarried woman was traveling alone with an unmarried man.

Whether it was a compliment to his honor or an insult to her appeal, he couldn't say. He imagined it was more that everyone assumed they held no attraction for one another.

He looked over at her, with her long, sable hair flowing over her back and a smile on her face, and wondered if she held any attraction for him.

For he had noted her beauty on many occasions. Especially of late, despite his attempts to keep such unwelcome thoughts away.

He would never act upon it. Not just because he was betrothed to someone else and could not offer marriage after such a thing. But he respected her too much for a dalliance, and he knew they could not be anything more than friends. While not lowborn, she was not considered worthy of a laird's heir.

It was ridiculous for anyone to think him better in any

way. She was smart and compassionate. In fact, everything honorable about him had come about from being her friend. He was certain of it.

That line between them had been there all their lives. Silently lurking. They may have pretended it didn't exist, but it remained. He feared one day soon that line between them would rise up and become a wall.

That would be a sad day indeed.

*

Despite Ella's worry for her aunt, she had been excited about the trip to Kildary since the moment her father had told her Kieran would escort her.

After reading Jenny's letter for herself, Ella was even less worried for her sturdy aunt. It seemed Jenny mentioned having an ague that had kept her resting rather than going to the Ross games at the castle.

Knowing Jenny as Ella did, she may have exaggerated the illness to get out of the festivities.

Of course, Ella said nothing of this to her father because she enjoyed visiting her aunt. And she surely wouldn't mind spending time alone with Kieran either.

As they rode out of the castle gates, she wondered if this would be the last time she and Kieran would be together like this.

While no one batted an eye that he would escort her alone, it wouldn't be acceptable after he was wed. Not that Ella imagined he'd be available for such things. No doubt his new wife would keep him wrapped up tight in her bed.

Ella certainly would.

She felt her cheeks turn warm at the thought, the memories from her dreams coming unbidden to her mind. She glanced over at the man next to her. She saw her best friend. And when he smiled, she saw the boy she'd grown up with. But he was no longer a boy.

He was a warrior if she'd ever seen one, with muscles along his arms that twitched from the smallest movement as he adjusted the reins or brushed back a lock of his overlong midnight hair.

"Why are you staring? Has a bird shite on my back again?" he asked, scrunching up his nose in disgust. God save her, the man was even enticing when he spoke of bird shite.

Her lust was fortunately replaced with laughter at the memory. Even if only momentarily.

"You are the worst friend," he said without heat. In fact, his lips pulled up on one side in a reluctant smile.

"I have apologized for that many times over the years. Perhaps you are an even worse friend for bringing it up over and over and not honoring the forgiveness you so gallantly offered."

"Mayhap it would be easier to accept your apologies if you wouldn't laugh when you extended them. I would be a fool to believe you held any true regret."

It was true enough, she had laughed at this incident as well as the day she'd pushed him on his arse. God save her, she was laughing now just thinking of it.

"I surely didn't *make* the bird shite on you. I canna conjure up a bird and instruct it where to leave its droppings. I know you accuse me of being a witch, but I do not hold control over the creatures that fly about the sky."

"No, only those that slither upon the ground," he teased.

How odd this moment was. So simple as to be forgotten immediately, but she couldn't because it was these times when she felt closest to Kieran. She couldn't allow it to be forgotten when he moved on with his life.

She'd done her best to keep distance from him recently, but now she thought better of her plan to save her heart. She didn't want to waste a moment of time with him.

She wondered, again, what would come of her. She hadn't realized how intertwined their lives had become. She talked to him every day. And had done so for so many years.

Even when one of them was ill and the other was told to stay a distance away to avoid catching, they still sat outside the other's door to chat and worry over the other.

And now they would be expected to just stop.

He would have another to turn to. Mayhap he wouldn't even notice Ella was gone. Would she be so easily swapped out for someone else? Perhaps it was this fear that worried her the most.

Well, that and the gaping dark nothingness she saw before her. Kieran may not like that he was being forced to marry, but at least his future was written out. He knew what to expect.

Ella had no idea what to do with the rest of her days. Would she just sit in her cottage, thinking about the time a bird shite on Kieran and doing her best to grasp on to the memory of his laughter?

While he lived would she simply just exist?

Nay, she needed to find something for herself. And soon.

But for now, she could properly grieve for what she was about to lose.

"I will miss this," she said without thinking.

He frowned at her. "Do you have something to tell me? Are you not planning to come back with me? Do you intend to stay on at Kildary with your aunt?" He frowned and reined his horse to a stop. "If this is your plan, I want to know. For I'd sooner turn around right now before we've even left

Sinclair lands rather than continue on knowing I'll have to say goodbye to my dearest friend."

Dearest friend. It was an honor to be his dearest friend, and yet not enough.

"Nay. But it soon will not matter where I live. After you marry, I will remain in the village and you'll reside in Castle Girnigoe with your wife, and we'll only see each other for festivals."

"I come into the kitchens nearly every day to nab a tart. You'll still be there, won't you?"

She couldn't tell him that she wouldn't. Even if she stayed with the Sinclairs, she wouldn't be able to be at the castle. Even the thought of seeing him with his wife at his side twisted her stomach into knots.

But for now, she would go on as if everything was fine.

"I suppose," she said, knowing it was probably a lie. "But as you age, you'll need to resist the tarts so not to go soft in your middle."

He patted his firm flat stomach. "Never."

He flashed his bright smile, and she felt another fracture in her heart.

How would she ever survive what was to come?

Chapter Eight

When the sun was near to gone, Kieran turned into the forest to find a place for them to stay for the night. Fortunately, it was warm enough they'd not need a fire, for they were passing through Oliphant lands.

They weren't at war with the clan, but the laird was a cruel man with a short temper, and the warriors Kieran had known had lacked honor. It wouldn't take much to fuel them into fighting if he was found alone.

Kieran found a clear spot near the edge of a ravine. An outcropping of rocks on their other side would keep them well hidden.

They'd brought dried meat and bannocks for their meal so they didn't need to cook anything. They could sleep until light and move on to make it to Kildary the next day.

Ellie spread out her bedroll much too close to his for his liking. He understood if she took a chill, it would be better to share his heat, but just the thought of being so close to her while lying down made his body stir.

Kieran pulled the meat and bannocks from his bag, and Ella held up a bit of cheese and two tarts.

"I thought you had taken to worry over my middle," he teased.

"Nay. I'll not have to look at ye naked, so what do I care if you enjoy your tarts?" She surely meant it as a jest, but the thought of her looking upon him naked stole the breath he needed to laugh.

His mind offered other thoughts unbidden. Ella's small hand on his taut stomach and moving lower.

He cleared his throat and thanked her for her contributions to their meal.

"We should get some rest. We'll be leaving as soon as it's light enough to see."

It was a mistake. He should have given himself time to get his body under control before having to lay out next to her. But it was too late to change course now.

She was so close he felt her warm breath on his arm.

She was on her side facing him, while he remained on his back looking up at the stars rather than look at her.

"Don't you find it strange that no one so much as blinks an eye that we would travel alone, the two of us overnight?"

"We've done such many times before. Why would anyone blink?" he asked, though he knew why.

"Am I so unladylike you forget I'm a woman?"

He turned his head to look at her but kept his body where it was.

"Of course, I know you're a woman, Ellie. I didn't mean that," he said, hoping to soothe her pique. "It's just if anything were going to happen between us, I imagine they think it would already be too late. You know a few assume such between us already."

"I feel as if we might as well take advantage of the situation if others assume it happens anyway."

He was sure her words were not meant to be taken seriously. Ella often spoke boldly with him, knowing he would not judge her for it. But the moment seemed to be stuck, the words lingering heavily between them.

Did she really want such a thing with him, or was she just airing empty thoughts? How would he ask? To do so would mean to admit he was interested in such a thing. Was he?

Of course, he was interested. He was a man who had never taken the opportunity to lie with a woman before. He thought about the act nearly every night and had to take himself in hand to keep from going mad with wanting it.

But with Ellie? Aye. On more than several occasions, she'd played the role of his lover in his fantasies. It seemed to reason since she was the only woman he knew so well.

But fantasies were not meant to be lived.

As the silence wore on while he struggled for something to say, Kieran was distracted by the sound of a twig snapping and the horses shifting nervously.

His instincts took over, and he pulled Ella closer so he could whisper in her ear. "Someone is close by. I will take the horses some distance away, you remain here by the rocks. Don't move or make a sound until I return."

He felt her nod, her silky hair tickling his nose with the movement. But there was no time to dwell on the scent of her. He rose to his feet with the practiced silence of a warrior, sliding his weapons into place before he made his way to the horses.

Untying them from the branch where they were held, he guided them away from where Ella was hidden.

He would not be able to leave Ella for very long. It meant he would not be able to lead the men far away. He would need to head them off and face them.

Circling around the sounds of footsteps in the forest, he made it seem as if he were coming from the other direction when he intercepted the four men.

Three men and one lad. If it came to fighting, he might have a chance.

"Ho there," the shorter, stockier man called.

Kieran held up his hand in greeting, though he wasn't sure they could see him in the darkness with only the moonlight seeping through the trees.

"Good eve, I am Kieran Sinclair, just passing through to home."

"Kieran Sinclair. What would have the laird's heir out alone in the night? I'd assume ye would travel with a dozen retainers." The men chuckled at their clansman's joke.

"The Sinclairs and the Oliphant are at peace, so I have no need for extra protection. Unless I am wrong on that?"

Kieran placed his hand on the hilt of the dirk on his belt. His daggers were lined up the leather sash across his chest that spanned the width of his back and held his sword. His muscles bunched at the ready.

One aggressive move from them would launch him into action.

"Seems ye have more horses than ye have arses to ride them."

Kieran nodded. "Aye, is often the way when I'm

bound for home after having delivered my burden."

The men looked him over, then they turned to the man who had spoken as if waiting for him to give the word.

"Mayhap you wish to leave one of them behind to ensure safe passage."

Kieran reached up and slowly slid his blade from his back.

"I've other means to ensure safe passage, if it were to come to that."

"Ye think you could take us all?" The man chuckled as if he hadn't a doubt he would live through the night.

Kieran took his time as he examined each man before giving a slow nod and a steady, "Aye."

There was restless movement from their quarter, but none had drawn a weapon.

"But if ye wish to act, I'd ask ye to get on with it, for I'm late for my bed and wish to be home." He slid one of his smaller blades and flipped it casually between his fingers. Hoping the display of his skill with a blade would deter them enough to give up on this farce.

Despite his calm outward appearance, he was tensed and ready on the inside. His mind had formulated a plan. The largest of the group would need to go down with a blade to his throat. Kieran hoped the lad would be scared off on sight. If not, he would wound him. The thin man would be taken down with Kieran's blade. And then he would face the leader, who would only fight if his other men were bested. He seemed round and slow from laziness.

Kieran thought of Ellie's prediction of what would happen to his middle if he ate too many tarts. Perhaps this lout had a best friend who supplied him tarts, but Kieran guessed his girth was likely due to drink.

"Seems a lot to lose for the possibility of two horses," Kieran added.

Kieran was waiting for the leader to act, so he was caught off guard when the thin man raised his sword and came at him first.

Kieran countered with his sword, taking the man down easily. The pudgy leader had drawn his sword as well, and Kieran flicked his blade into his neck, and he dropped a foot from Kieran's boot.

The largest man and the lad didn't move. They hadn't drawn their weapons. Still, Kieran waited to see if they planned to.

The lad turned to the man. "What do we do, da?"

"I'll not lose ye for a bit of horseflesh."

"It seems you've gained two extra horses as it is," Kieran said, nodding toward the two bodies and the horses they'd left behind.

"Let's be on our way, Matty."

The two remaining men gathered the horses as Kieran collected his blade and wiped down his weapons hastily in the grass.

"You should not tarry on Oliphant lands, Sinclair. 'Tis not safe."

And even less so now that Kieran had slain two of their men.

With the power of battle still rushing through Kieran's veins, he almost asked the man who exactly would not be safe, but he held his tongue, not wanting to make the situation more heated.

"Thank ye. I wish ye well."

He took up the reins and led the horses onward, which was in the direction of where he'd come from, where Ellie was hiding.

He moved slow enough and listened to make sure the man and his son had ridden off in the other direction before he went to find Ellie.

She was shaking as if with a chill, despite the warm evening.

"Are you well?" he asked.

She startled and then rushed toward him, wrapping her arms around his waist. He wound his own arms around her, holding her close.

"I was worried about you," she said. "But you always

protect me."

He nodded and pressed his face to her hair, breathing in the scent of her. Home, happiness, and laughter.

"Always," he promised, though as the word echoed into the night air, he realized he would not be called on to protect her much longer.

*

They stood there in the darkness holding one another. Ella could feel the pounding of Kieran's heart, as was common for warriors after battle.

Her father had told her how exhausting it was to fight someone. The energy one carried into a conflict was often drained completely in just a few minutes of war.

Ella had heard the short skirmish from her hiding place. She hadn't been able to make out the words, but she'd heard a few raised voices, the scrape of metal, and the thud of a body falling to the damp earth.

Kieran's strong arms pulled her closer to him, and she felt his arousal between them.

It was what she had wanted when she'd so carelessly suggested they take advantage of being left alone, but now the idea frightened her.

Not Kieran. She'd never be afraid of him.

But she'd heard soldiers complain about finding a lass to calm their battle lust after a fight and assumed it happened to all men.

Kieran was a man, so it would serve he would have the same response.

She didn't want him to be with her because of some physical need or response to the brief threat on his life. She wanted him to want her because he could not go on without being with her.

She found the needed courage to back away from him.

She cleared her dry throat before speaking in as light a tone as she could muster.

"We should probably get some sleep before the sun comes up."

"Aye." He shrugged out of his weapons belt and sash, setting them close at hand. Always the ready soldier.

This time when they settled on their furs, he turned his back to her.

She raised her hand and reached across the darkness, wanting to touch his warm skin, but her earlier courage had faded. Instead, she dropped her hand and lay there listening to his breathing until sleep found her.

Hours later, when the sun hinted at the horizon, she woke to find he was already up and had watered the horses. The uncomfortable silence was gone, and they set out laughing and joking as they had the day before.

But Ella couldn't help but feel like a valuable opportunity had been missed. If she hadn't been afraid of rejection, she might have had all her questions answered and a memory to cherish for the rest of her life. Now, she would have to live knowing her chance was lost because she was not brave enough to take it.

Wiping away a silly tear, she asked Kieran for the details of his fight with the Oliphants.

He told her what had happened and what had been said. She marveled at the fact that Kieran did not spin a more elaborate tale as many of her father's soldiers did to make themselves sound like a better fighter than what they were.

She knew Kieran told only the bare facts. The way he led them around the area where she'd heard the fighting told her the men he'd bested still lay in the forest.

"We'll be to Kildary in a few hours."

"Should we sing?" she asked.

He looked over at her with wide eyes.

"Please, no. Between the two of us, we shall send the horses to madness, and we need them to get the rest of the way to the Ross lands."

"We are not so bad."

"I am not so bad, you are downright horrid, and I mean it in the nicest way as you are my best friend, but if you sing, I'll have no choice but to pull my blade across my own throat to end my misery."

"Very well, since I will need your escort back to Caithness after I see my aunt well, I will relent."

A few moments later she said, "Mayhap I could—"

"Nay. No humming either."

Sometimes having a friend who knew one so well was not such a wonderful thing.

Chapter Nine

They crested the hill that led to the village of Kildary. The Ross castle, Balnagown, stood on the opposite hill. Kieran would need to make his way there to greet the laird.

The Ross clan and the Sinclairs occasionally spent time raiding each other's cattle, but no real animosity lay between them. Kieran felt a shadow of disappointment that he wouldn't be called upon to marry a Ross for an alliance. He knew which Ross woman he would recommend for such a duty.

He dropped back, allowing Ellie to pick their path down the hill and through the cottages to the one she had visited in the past.

Kieran had always felt a bit of anger at Ellie's aunt for inviting her to stay with her a few weeks each summer. When Ellie had been away, he'd been alone, missing her. And when she'd returned with tales of her aunt and all the merriment they'd had, he'd been jealous.

He was grown now and was not so selfish to still be angry at the woman. But after helping Ellie down, he offered to see to their horses rather than follow her inside.

"I'll return after I've seen to our mounts."

"Thank you," she said almost dismissively before she rushed into the cottage.

He could tell Ellie had seemed more worried as they'd gotten closer to the village. Mainly because she'd grown quieter and had given up on her quest for them to sing or hum.

Kieran planned to give her some time with her aunt alone before joining them. The better for Ellie to determine how serious her aunt's illness was.

He headed toward the stables in the village and stopped when two women stepped out in front of his horse.

"Ladies," he greeted them with a smile even if he'd rather ask them to move so he might continue on.

"Who might ye be?"

"Kieran Sinclair."

"Sinclair?" The women shared a look. "Would you be

looking for company during your stay at Kildary?"

Kieran only hesitated a moment.

"Nay. I have company already. Thank ye, and good day."

Fortunately, they moved to the side so he might continue on.

Mayhap he should have taken them up on their offer so to deal with the issue of his virginity before he married. He just couldn't bring himself to swive a woman he didn't know at all. To use someone in that way didn't set well with him.

His new bride would just have to wait him out while he got his legs under him, as it were. How bad could he be?

He knew what was done. He would take his cues from her to know better how to please her. Long ago, Teague had told him about pleasuring a woman.

He was instructed to never be disrespectful and not to plant his seed anywhere he didn't wish it to grow. Looking back at the ladies who'd waved at him, he knew he didn't want to plant anything there.

He remembered the night before with Ellie so close he could feel the heat of her body. The way he'd woken with her snuggled up against him and how uncomfortably hard he'd been.

He'd managed to roll away and go take care of himself quickly down by the creek before washing and getting water for the horses.

He noticed the women who had flirted with him didn't make his blood rise the way Ellie's closeness had.

He could only hope his wife suited him in the same way. He surely didn't want to spend the rest of his days longing for Ellie Ross.

*

Ella entered the cottage, dark but for a low fire in the hearth, the furs pulled over the windows to block out the midafternoon light. A cough came from the bed, and Ella went to that side.

"Aunt, it's Ellisay. I've come to care for you."

"Ella?" Her aunt squinted. "He didn't tell me you were coming. I would have told him it wasn't necessary. I'm nearly over the illness. Only a bit of a cough left. I was just taking a rest. It's best for gaining strength, ye know."

"Aye." Her aunt had always said as much as the reason she needed a rest.

"Has your father brought ye?" The woman rose, and Ella hurried to the fire to light a rush so she could light the candles.

"Nay. The laird required him to stay at Girnigoe."

"Of course. The Sinclair laird canna wipe his own arse

without my brother's opinion on it."

Ella smiled at her aunt's blunt speaking. Jenny, the youngest daughter of the Ross laird, had never married despite her beauty. She chose to live alone in a cottage on the edge of the village rather than stay at Balnagown, which had once been her home.

Ella wondered if this would be her fate as well. Once Kieran married, would Ella wish to hide away from life on her own? She wasn't ready to give up on finding her own bit of happiness.

"Speaking of lairds, how is Uncle William?" Ella asked. Her father's oldest brother was laird of the Ross clan. Being one of many nieces and nephews, Ella didn't know if her uncle would even recognize her if she bothered to visit him.

Aunt Jenny waved a hand.

"He's very important. That's all we need to know about him." Jenny rolled her eyes while pulling a brush through her brown hair. Her wavy locks were similar in shade to Ella's, with a few threads of silver where the red had once been.

Her aunt moved to stir up the fire, but Ella took the poker from her.

"I've come to help you, so sit and let me do it. I'll not report back to my da that I lazed about and let you serve me. I would be a disgrace."

Jenny chuckled.

"Very well, then. Fetch me my robe."

After stirring the fire back to life and adding a few logs for cooking and boiling water, Ella helped her aunt into the worn robe and pulled back the furs from the windows to let in the light and fresh air. The cottage seemed to come alive with happy memories as soon as the sun touched it.

Ella remembered the worn rugs on the floor and the sturdy chairs by the hearth where she'd spent many evenings listening to her aunt tell her tales of knights and princesses.

In her mind, the knights had always taken on the appearance of Kieran, and, of course, she thought of herself as the princess in the story.

She was straightening up and taking stock of her aunt's stores when someone rapped heavily on the door.

"That will be Kieran," Ellie said as she went to open the door. He ducked to enter because of his height and stood straighter once inside. She knew he was large, but he looked all the more so for standing in the tiny room.

"This is the mighty Kieran I've heard so much about over the years?" Aunt Jenny said.

Kieran flashed his white smile at the woman before offering a courtly bow, and Ella thought she saw the woman blush.

"When Ellisay would come to visit in the summers, it would be a full week before every sentence from her mouth didn't start with your name, lad. I had rather grown tired of hearing how wonderful you were."

Kieran laughed.

"I could say the same about ye upon her return to Caithness."

Ella held out the bucket, and Kieran took it without complaint to go fill it at the well.

When he had left, Aunt Jenny turned to her with a sly smile.

"Your lad has grown into a handsome man."

"He isn't my lad," Ella said, hiding the sadness that truth brought to her. "He is to be married after harvest."

"But not to you?"

Ella laughed. "Nay. The Sinclair heir must marry well. Not to someone like me."

"You were a laird's granddaughter and now a laird's niece."

"I am of no consequence, and you well know it. There is no alliance to come from marrying me. No riches or lands. Do you think Uncle William would agree to stop thieving the Sinclair stock for my sake?"

"Ye know well enough he is only stealing back his own cattle."

"And I'm sure the Sinclairs think they are doing the same. Which is probably why the wee altercations have never grown into war between the clans. And no war means no need of an alliance." Ella shrugged, doing her best not to allow her disappointment to show. Hopefully, her aunt wouldn't notice how much thought she'd put into such a possible arrangement.

Jenny made an unhappy noise and brushed it off with a wave of her hand. As if these things didn't matter in the Highlands. As if they weren't the only things that mattered for anyone who would have the honor of marrying Kieran.

"It doesn't matter. Kieran and I are friends. That is all that has ever been between us and all that I can hope will remain after he weds."

Ella recalled the night before, when he'd held her and she'd felt his body respond to her. The thought of him holding another in the same way nearly stole her breath.

She had often thought of Kieran as hers alone. But it had always been friendship. She'd not wanted him to leave her behind to play with the other boys, so she'd made sure to play what he wanted. But it was different now. It wasn't just friendship. She wanted him to be hers in every way.

Jenny frowned but said nothing else as Kieran entered again with the water.

"We'll need some things for our meal." Ellie gathered the basket by the door, and Kieran followed after her without being asked. She wasn't sure if she wanted him with her. But she also couldn't be sure she did not.

She didn't want to miss an opportunity to walk next to him as if she belonged there, but she also knew from the look on her aunt's face that it would be unlikely they would remain friends after he married.

She should go alone so as to get used to such a future, but instead she said nothing and allowed him to make the decision to come along with her.

They stopped to purchase vegetables and a plump chicken for the stew she would make. As they were leaving, a young girl came up selling bundles of heather.

"For your lady," the girl said to Kieran.

Ella opened her mouth to explain, but Kieran simply put a coin in the girl's hand. Ella looked up at him in surprise, and he shrugged as if it was not something worth note. To her, it was everything.

She thought of how their lives might be if she were his lady. When he would be laird and they would rule the Sinclair clan together. It had not been something she'd thought of during all her woolgathering about her friend.

She had not been trained to be a lady; in fact, she was rather the opposite. She didn't know what was expected of a laird's wife, for there had not been a lady overseeing Girnigoe Castle in all her days.

Surely, the lady of the keep would be responsible for managing the castle as well as the staff. She'd be required to see to the household ledgers and the larders.

Not to mention entertain guests and see to their comfort.

She didn't know the first thing about entertaining guests or how much food stores were needed to keep the castle fed for the winter. Dara had always taken care of such things. But she bet the MacKenzie lass had been brought up to know all these things.

Had Ella thought she would make Kieran a better wife? Ella realized now she was not suitable in any of the ways that mattered.

Chapter Ten

Kieran couldn't understand what had changed. It seemed a small thing, a straggly bundle of flowers. But Ellie's face had lit up, and her eyes had gone soft. When she'd smiled at him, there was no hint of her usual mischief. No tilt of her lips that spoke of years of shared secrets between them.

This smile nearly stole his breath and knocked him from his feet.

He'd considered for a moment to tell her the truth, that he'd thought it would be a nice thing to do for her aunt. Something to brighten up her day after being ill. But after seeing the look on Ellie's face, he wouldn't dare.

He'd stumbled into this situation that had her looking

at him as if he'd hung the moon in the sky. And he'd selfishly take every moment while it was his.

He found himself wishing he could go back to before he'd been betrothed. Back when Ellie had just been his friend and nothing more.

If he had the freedoms he'd had then, he would have picked her flowers to make her look at him in such a way on purpose.

And then he would have been able to pull her into his arms and kiss her the way he'd been thinking of doing for the last several days.

Why had he waited so long to realize how he'd felt about her?

Now it was too late. He would be married in a few months, and he worried he would spend the rest of his life wishing for Ellie.

What a wretched life that would be.

He opened the door to the cottage and allowed her to go in first. For a second's time he paused, thinking it might be better not to follow her. To cut their ties now and run away.

But looking at the scar on his palm, he knew he'd never be able to cut their ties.

Fortunately, Jenny was there to distract Ellie from looking at him as her knight in shining armor, while also distracting him from his thoughts of what he wished he could do with his friend.

Jenny and Ellie put him to work.

After helping Ellie with the meal in which she called it *helping*, though he just felt in the way while watching her, they sat to eat. Ellie's Aunt Jenny spent most of the meal asking questions.

Ellie answered most of them. Even the ones meant for him. But Ellie knew everything about him, so it was easy enough for him to relax into the meal with a few nods and little effort on his part.

"I shall take my leave of you, ladies, and go up to the castle to bunk down for the night. I'll see you in the morning."

Jenny huffed. "I doubt that."

She probably thought he would spend the night in drink, as was common with warriors. But Kieran had never taken to it, preferring to have his mornings clear. In the times he had overindulged, he'd found himself wishing he'd just die and get it over with. That was no way to go through life.

In the castle, the people in the great hall were just finishing their meal and some were settling for the evening entertainments. Kieran made his way to the high table and easily identified the laird seated in the center with his wife next to him.

Bowing, he introduced himself.

"My laird, it is an honor to make your acquaintance. I

am Kieran Sinclair. Heir to the Sinclair laird. I've escorted your niece Ellisay to visit her Aunt Jenny, and I ask permission to sleep in the hall with your warriors if you would be so kind."

"Kieran? Rolfe's son?"

"Aye," he answered, though he never truly felt like Rolfe's son. That position had been for Brody and had remained empty since his death. Kieran hadn't managed to fill the space left by his older brother.

"We can offer better accommodations than the hall for the Sinclair heir." He whispered to his wife, who stood.

"I don't want to cause any inconvenience." Kieran held up his hands.

"It is not an inconvenience to honor a guest appropriately."

Kieran nodded and turned to the woman who was leaving. "I thank ye, mistress."

He caught her appraising glance and turned away, hoping her husband hadn't noticed. He would bar his door tonight so as not to have unwanted visitors. Especially those that would cause him to find his head unattached from his body.

The laird offered him his wife's now-vacant seat and introduced him to the other men sitting at the high table.

"Arran Sutherland is my war chief." The laird nodded

toward a large man who looked much too happy to call his clan to war. Kieran knew Teague was a kind man, but upon meeting him no one would think it for his surly countenance. This man, close to Kieran's age, wore a big smile that spoke of friendliness.

"Good to meet ye," Arran said. "Do ye wish to train with us in the morning?"

"The morning?" Kieran couldn't hide his surprise.

"Aye. I put an end to drinking in excess every night when I took over as war chief last year."

Kieran smiled.

"The Sinclair war chief did the same many years ago."

"That is wise," the laird said before leaning closer to whisper, "some of my men don't have much in wits; I need to be sure they keep what they have."

They laughed.

Arran explained further. "There was an attack on the castle in the early hours of the morning when all the men were still asleep and useless. The war chief was killed, and the laird brought me on to make sure nothing of the like ever happened again."

Kieran nodded. 'Twas the same reason Teague insisted his men remain sober. Even during feasts, not all of the men took part.

A tankard of ale was placed before Kieran by a

smiling maid, and he thanked her.

"So how is my brother?" the laird asked.

The rest of the evening was spent talking and laughing. Kieran heard many stories he would use against Teague at the next opportunity.

The laird's young sons joined them for a while. They were at that gangly age where they hadn't yet grown into their large feet, but the laird offered praise. It was clear he was proud of the three lads.

Kieran felt himself wondering what that might be like. To have a father who loved him. To have had a man like Laird Ross as a father must have been wonderful. Really, any father would have likely been better than his own.

Rolfe had never hurt Kieran. He'd never hit him or even yelled all that much. But Kieran wondered if it was because the man didn't care enough about Kieran to bother with such things.

Many times, Kieran thought mayhap he just wasn't worth the man's effort.

Two young ladies sang a few songs, and Kieran's thoughts turned to Ellie and how she sang like a cat being attacked.

When the entertainments were over, he was led to a large room that was well appointed with sturdy furniture and a view of the loch.

He had just reached for the buckle on his weapons belt when a soft knock stopped him.

Upon opening the door, he faced one of the lasses with the angel's voice who had sung for them that evening. He knew who she was, but he didn't know why she was knocking on his door so late.

His breath caught when he realized he did know why she was there.

"Did ye wish for company this evening?" she asked with a hopeful smile.

He knew, as heir, many women hoped to latch on to him so they could one day be lady of the castle.

"I'm betrothed," he said and watched as disappointment colored her face.

"I see. Then good night to ye."

"And to you," he said to her retreating form. The door closed, and he pulled the bar across it.

He may not have a choice in who he wed, but at least he wouldn't be lured into marriage by someone who only wanted to use him to ensure her power.

Kieran frowned to think his mother had been such a woman. One who had cruelly tricked a grieving widower into sleeping with her so he would offer marriage. And then, when that wasn't enough, she had allowed his cherished child to be taken by the sea.

It was no wonder Kieran's father hated his mother for what she'd done and how she'd ruined the man's life.

But Kieran had done nothing. Why was he charged with her crimes?

He went to bed thinking of his mother as the woman who had come to his room, and while his dreams were filled with frustration and anger, he was saved for one night at least to not have to dream of Ellie.

The next morning, Kieran met up with Arran and the men in the bailey as they began their drills.

Before long, they were working up a sweat and tunics came off to allow for ease of movement. It wasn't uncommon for warriors to do such in the bailey. It was a way of castle life.

What Kieran hadn't experienced was a group of women gathering in the bailey to watch the men.

"Do they not have work to do?" Kieran asked the chief.

"Ach, aye, they do, but I welcome them to come and watch the men," Arran said like it was a common thing.

"Why would ye do that?" Kieran was fit of form and a good fighter. He didn't have anything to be embarrassed about, yet it was uncomfortable to be gawked at like a prized pig to be roasted for supper.

"It makes the men work harder to impress the lasses. It's the best motivation I've found for getting my men to work harder and longer without a word of complaint."

Kieran looked about at the men and noticed they had picked up their pace.

"I shouldn't have doubted your methods," Kieran laughed.

"It's not only about the drills. Some of the men have made matches this way. The two red-haired lasses over there are married to two of my warriors. Even the married men like to impress their wives at drills. The men who aren't married often earn comforts from the women who gather. If you are interested, I can tell ye which are spoken for and which are available."

"Nay," Kieran said immediately. "That is, I am betrothed and will be married in a few months."

"Ah. Love will keep ye honest, then."

Kieran should have just let it go, but he corrected Arran instead.

"Nay, I've never met her. My father made an alliance with her father."

Arran shook his head. "I can't imagine being married to a complete stranger. You've never even seen her?"

Kieran shrugged. "I knew this was what my future held. I'm not happy about it, and no, I haven't seen her. Nor do I know anything about her other than her name. But it is my duty."

Arran slapped him on the shoulder.

"I wish the best for ye. I hope your bride is bonny and kind."

"Thank ye." Kieran lifted his sword again and thought about his intended and if she would be bonny and kind. He found himself wishing she were mischievous and witty instead. For that would better fill his life with happiness.

Looks faded when age took hold, and kindness seemed rather boring as life trudged on. He'd rather have someone to challenge him. Someone who would tease him and whom he would devil in return.

And damn if he didn't find himself thinking of Ellie again.

Chapter Eleven

After breaking their fast, Jenny announced she wanted to get out of her cottage. Ella was happy to oblige, having spent the night restlessly while thinking of Kieran.

She couldn't help but feel she had both lost an opportunity and avoided a mistake with him. Which was ridiculous. It couldn't be both. Could it?

"I've been cooped up inside for too long, and I want to walk about with the sun on my face."

"Da will be pleased I seemed to have healed you from your illness in just one night."

Jenny laughed as she gathered her basket.

"My brother worries too much. If I had been so ill, I wouldn't have wasted my strength to write to him about such mundane things as going riding and getting caught in the rain. Which I'm sure is how I caught a chill."

"I thought your illness a timely convenience if one wished to avoid the games at the castle." Ella looked straight ahead with only a small smile on her lips.

"You have grown wise, niece. I'll say you take after me in that way."

"Why do you not live at the castle, as is your right?"

"I grew weary of castle life and even more weary of the expectations inside those walls."

"You speak of marriage?"

"Aye. Though I'm too old for my brother, the laird, to bind me to someone in an alliance, I wouldn't put it past him if he noticed some visitor taking an interest in me."

"Would that be so bad? To marry?"

"When one has given their heart to another, it is an impossible thing. Sure to bring nothing but pain to the person unlucky enough to be snared to a heartless bride."

Ella frowned. She'd often thought herself similar to her aunt. Both had a pleasant character with a hearty sense of humor. She didn't realize they were alike in this way as well.

She wondered if she might be able to confide in her aunt about her growing feelings for Kieran. But she didn't want to hear the truth Aunt Jenny would no doubt bestow upon her. Ella wasn't ready to give up on her fantasies.

Jenny cleared her throat and pressed her lips into a smile.

"It is nice that my wee brother cares enough to look after me."

Ella nodded, knowing her father worried over Jenny. He had asked her many times to move to Caithness with them. But Jenny always replied that she liked being on her own.

Yet every time Ella visited, Jenny seemed lonely.

Her father had once said Jenny would probably never live with them while they lived on Sinclair lands, but he'd never said why. And maybe Ella had never asked.

"Auntie, do you have an issue with the Sinclairs?" she asked now.

Jenny's smile dropped immediately, and she shook her head with more vigor than a simple denial.

"Why would I care one way or another about the Sinclairs?"

Kieran often answered her questions with other questions when he was trying to avoid answering her. It seemed Jenny had mastered the technique as well.

"I didn't say you would care at all about the Sinclairs, but we live in Caithness; it would be easy enough for you to live there with us."

"I like my freedom."

"As you've said. You wouldn't need to live in our

cottage. You could live in your own home, just close enough that we could see each other more often." It would have been nice having a woman around when she was younger and her body and emotions seemed to have taken over.

"I'm settled here." She waved the basket around at the village.

In previous visits, Jenny had introduced her to some of the villagers, but Ella wouldn't have called them dear friends of her aunt. She wasn't particularly close to her brother, the laird. From what Ella could tell, Jenny rarely even visited the castle. And had clearly used her illness to get out of attending the games.

Ella would remember to ask her father about it when she returned home. She didn't like Jenny living here alone. Not that she was too old to care for herself—she was fit and independent.

But then Ella remembered why it might be better for her aunt to stay here in Kildary. So Ella might have a place to live if she found it too difficult to stay at home after Kieran married.

After yesterday, when he'd gotten her flowers, it was easy to pretend they would still be friends.

She hadn't forgotten her world was about to shift, but she rather wished she could.

*

Arran Sutherland was a good chief and a good fighter. Kieran knew so by how his body ached after drills were completed. He'd used muscles Teague must have missed in recent months. But it was a good thing, and he'd not complain.

"Do ye wish to head into the village for a dram and a meat pie?" Arran asked.

"Nay. I must check in with my friend. She is caring for her aunt, and I should see if they need any help."

"I'll come with you. We can see to the ladies quickly and still go to the village."

Kieran agreed to this plan. A half-dozen meat pies would not be amiss after training as they had. Kieran tugged his clothes back on after a dip in the loch and led Arran toward Jenny's cottage.

The man chatted easily about this and that.

It was odd having a male friend, but he thought he could count Arran as such. Or at least until they'd entered Jenny's cottage and Arran's gaze fell upon Ellie.

Kieran worried the man's tongue might spill from his mouth.

"Arran Sutherland, the Ross war chief," Kieran introduced him. "This is Ellisay Ross, niece to the Ross laird. And you've probably met her aunt Jenny."

"I've heard of Jenny, but we've not met. It is a pleasure to meet you both," Arran said, though his gaze never moved from Ellie.

Kieran expected Ellie to narrow her eyes on the man, as he'd seen her do many times when she'd received unwanted attention. But to his surprise, she smiled at Arran in a most becoming way. The way he'd only ever seen her smile at him.

Something ugly stirred in his chest, and he fought the urge to grab hold of his new friend and toss him from the cottage on his arse. Kieran was not so daft to not realize what the feeling was.

He just didn't expect to feel it so fervently. Ellie was not his. She was free to smile at other men. He only wished he didn't have to witness it.

"I didn't realize my kin was no longer the war chief. I wonder why my da didn't tell me," Ellie said.

"I believe the laird reached out to Teague to offer him the position when it became available, but he turned it down. I'm rather glad for it. It gave me an opportunity here despite my age."

"I didn't know that," Kieran said. "Teague never said." Kieran wondered why Teague would stay as chief with the Sinclairs when he could have come home and been the chief for his own clan.

"He didn't tell me either," Ellie said with a shrug.

"Please have a seat. I made tarts. I know Kieran won't be able to pass them up. Tell me, Arran, is your stomach your master as well?"

"Aye. At least until I find some fetching lass to serve instead."

What was this? Were they flirting? Kieran didn't know this Arran well enough, but he knew Ellie, and she didn't flirt. He didn't even know she knew how to.

Clearly, she had gotten her talent for secrecy from her father.

"We only came to see if you needed anything before we went into the village to—"

"Surely, we wouldn't want to miss out on freshly made tarts. The village will be there another time," Arran said quickly and offered a courtly bow to Ellie. "We would be honored."

Ellie laughed. Nay, she didn't laugh, she giggled. A tinkling, frail little sound made by dainty women being trained to lure a husband. Ellie had never made such a sound in her life, he was sure of it. But then, mayhap there were things he didn't know about his best friend.

She surely didn't know everything about him. Like how that silly laugh had affected him or how much he wanted to pull his dirk if Arran took another step closer to her.

Jenny didn't help matters as she asked Arran a litany

of questions. Most were strategic inquiries set to determine whether or not Arran had a wife or was promised to anyone. Both were answered as no.

"I do hope to marry someday," Arran said, not taking his gaze from Ellie. Kieran felt his hand twitch as he fought the instinct to punch his new friend in the face.

Had he thought this man a friend earlier? Now he seemed a threat to Kieran's true friend.

And why were these tarts so bloody dry? He could hardly manage to swallow them. Perhaps it was the hideous lump in his throat.

It was a shock to see no one seemed to notice Kieran's reaction. He did better at hiding it than he would have thought. Eventually, Kieran managed to relax and let go of his anger. Or at least loosened his grip a bit.

Kieran knew Arran hadn't done anything to earn his fury. In truth, Kieran could even see how the chief and Ellie would be well suited, both having a keen sense of humor.

And wouldn't it be better if Ellie found someone for herself before Kieran married, so neither of them would be alone? The less selfish part of him wanted only for Ellie's happiness with whomever she found it.

But another part of him, a part he had hidden even from himself, wanted to call out, "Mine."

"You did not tell me your friend was so fetching,

Kieran," Arran said, still not looking at him. "And a fair baker as well."

"It has only taken twenty years of practice. I've been forced to sample Ellie's disast—"

"Ella," Ellie corrected him, widening her eyes in some manner of communication he didn't understand. Which was an odd sensation since he was always well attuned to every shift in her thoughts.

"What?"

"Ella. You know I haven't been called Ellie since I was a lass."

Kieran blinked and looked about the table. He'd called her Ellie yesterday and every day before that. He'd noticed her father had taken to calling her Ella, and so had her aunt.

Had he missed her telling him she preferred Ella? Perhaps she had and he'd ignored her request. He hadn't thought of her as Ella before. She'd always been *Ellie*, the girl who followed him everywhere in breeches. The lass who dared him to jump from the stable roof and then ran for help when that had proved a bad idea.

Ellie snorted when she laughed at his outrageous jokes and stood up to boys larger than herself as if she didn't realize how small she was. Ellie spit and cursed, and she was part of him.

Ella sounded like a stranger. Someone who flirted and

giggled.

This woman in front of him now, this alluring vixen, was definitely an Ella. He wanted to go to her and capture her lips with his. She had grown up. He knew as much, he had watched it happen before his eyes, but he only now saw her.

Ella.

Rather than risk losing control of himself, he suggested he and Arran carry out their earlier plans to visit the village. Arran reluctantly agreed, but eventually they were out of the cottage. The fresh air and the distance from Ellie— Ella—seemed to clear his head, but Kieran had seen the beast lurking in the shadows of his soul.

And worse, he was aware of what it was and why it had come at that moment.

Jealousy had never risen up in him with such vengeance before. Taunting him with possible futures where Ella married Arran. Grew round, had his children, and gave him her smiles. He saw a happy life for them, while he wasted away at Girnigoe with a faceless stranger, living out his days wishing Ella was *his*.

"Is she promised to anyone?" Arran asked as they walked about the village. Despite them just having tarts and ale at Jenny's, they made quick work of a few meat pies as well.

"Nay," Kieran managed to wrestle the truth through

his lips, though he fought the urge to lie. To keep this man from moving forward with his obvious plans to consider Ella for his wife.

"She is lovely," Arran said.

"Aye. It's strange, I don't think I had noticed how lovely she is until just recently. She's been my best friend all my life. I have few memories that don't include her in some manner."

Arran stopped walking and placed his hand on Kieran's arm, a look of compassion on his face.

"Do ye love her, then? You're to marry someone else, but you want Ella?"

"Nay," Kieran answered quickly. Mayhap too quickly. For he wasn't certain he'd answered correctly.

Arran tilted his head, and Kieran wanted more than anything for the man to stop staring at him. He didn't want this man who may one day call Ella his to see the truth Kieran himself had not known.

He wanted Ella for himself.

Bloody hell.

Chapter Twelve

"My, my," Jenny had said as soon as the door closed behind the men. "I will attempt to fall ill more often so you'll have need to visit and lure the strapping young warriors to my cottage."

Ella still felt the heat on her cheeks from her aunt's teasing, which hadn't stopped since.

"Which one do you find more handsome?" Jenny asked sometime later.

"One of them doesn't count. Kieran is only a friend." Or he had been. Ella had found Arran handsome indeed. In fact, on looks alone, one might argue Arran was the more handsome of the two. Kieran's black hair was rather long and a bit shaggy. While Arran kept his golden-brown hair trimmed to curl invitingly at his ears.

Arran's voice was not so deep, and his words were full of flattery.

But it was Kieran who made her heart flutter.

"I wouldn't be so sure that Kieran is only a friend. I saw the way he watched you while you flirted with Arran."

"I wasn't flirting. I don't even know how to go about such a thing." Except she had seemed flirtatious. Perhaps it was a skill that came out only when faced with a man who flirted with her. Arran had flirted. He'd been intriguing. And mayhap most important, he wasn't promised to marry someone else.

He had a warm smile and an infectious laugh. It would not be a hardship to grow old listening to that laugh.

"And even if I was, by some chance, flirting with Arran, Kieran wouldn't care. He is betrothed."

Jenny tilted her head. "Some men are not content with one lass."

Ella laughed. "I can assure you, Kieran would never betray his vows."

"Ah, maybe not, but he's not spoken any vows yet, has he?"

Ella thought of the day before, when he'd bought her

flowers, and let out a sigh. It wouldn't do to want Kieran as more than a friend, for he was not to be hers.

"Arran was charming, and more importantly, he is available," Ella spoke her earlier thoughts aloud. Maybe more for herself than her aunt.

"Maybe so, but I know well enough that one cannot simply make do with the one that is available."

Ella tilted her head, taking in the sadness that came over her aunt's expression.

"What happened, aunt?" Ella asked, knowing easily her aunt was remembering something unsettling.

"It was a long time ago. I was even younger than you. I thought myself in love with a man who was visiting Balnagown. My father was laird, and while I was the third daughter, I would still have been considered an honorable match. I fell victim to his charms immediately. No one had ever looked at me the way he did. I gave him my heart, among other things."

She frowned, and Ella's hands clenched into fists, wanting to seek vengeance on this man who took Jenny's virtue and left her brokenhearted.

"My father didn't allow us in the hall, so I knew nothing of clan business or why Roger was visiting. It wasn't until the wedding was being planned that I learned Roger was the MacKinnon laird and had come to marry my eldest sister."

Ella gasped in surprise.

"Did Aunt Helen know what he did?"

Jenny shook her head. "Nay. It wouldn't have done her any good for her to know. Helen had no choice but to marry him. She was just as enamored by his charms as I was, and it would only hurt her to know he'd used me. It wasn't until Roger and Helen left that Rachel, my next older sister, told me he had seduced her as well."

"Good Lord, that rotten bastard."

"It's the way of men in power. They always get what they want. My own father was much the same. It is the reason Teague left. Your mother was lovely, and he worried one of his brothers or some lord who visited would claim her as his own."

"And his father would have allowed their marriage to be put aside because my da was not titled."

Jenny smiled sadly and nodded.

"William's second wife has given him three fine sons, and he is a good laird. He's not like my father. He'd never force anyone to marry."

Jenny looked away, the sadness back in her eyes, and Ella couldn't help herself.

"Roger was not worthy of this heartache. Even if you loved him, he doesn't deserve to take up so much of your time."

Jenny smiled and shook her head.

"I realized shortly after he left that I never loved him. But I did love another, and his heart was for someone else. It was only after I'd lost the second man I thought to call husband that I decided I would rather be alone than need a man for anything more than fetching me water. And for that, there is always a lad about who is eager for a coin." She smiled again, as if the shadow of sadness Ella had seen had never existed.

Ella didn't ask anything else.

She'd never noticed the divide between her world and Kieran's. They had been friends, equals for as long as she could remember. But, in truth, they were not equal. Kieran's future had been sealed from the time his older brother had died.

Things were going to change between them.

Ella needed to be prepared.

She needed to start thinking of her own future and what she wanted. What might make her happy. Or if not happy, at least not miserable.

Arran seemed like a fine man. He didn't rouse her heart to beating the way Kieran's had come to do, but mayhap it was better that way. She'd not be at risk for injuring her heart if it had no reason to get away from her.

*

Kieran barely slept the night before. Every time he closed his eyes, he pictured Ella with Arran, and as he tried to move forward to stop her from going away with him, he found his feet were chained to the castle wall.

Giving up, he went down to the hall to break his fast and was one of the first men in the bailey to start drills. Arran was already there, smiling, as was his way. Meanwhile, Kieran was having trouble mustering any hint of pleasantries.

As they began sparring, Kieran felt free to do what he could not do in his dreams.

"Might I remind you we are only sparring?" Arran said as he bent over to catch his breath. "You're going to have me on my arse."

Kieran had gone at the man with more effort than a mere practice session required, but he'd been angry and needed to work it out.

While he knew Arran was not the true cause of his foul mood, it seemed he would be the focus of it.

"I would like to invite Ellisay to the castle for the late meal. Do you think she would come?" Arran asked.

"She's here to see to her aunt, not dine in the hall with a bunch of ogling men."

"I didn't mean to ogle. But as I said yesterday, the lass

is lovely. Odd that no one has offered for her before. Is there something wrong with her?"

That remark had Kieran raising his blade. Arran backed away from the flailing sword, but the edge of Kieran's blade caught Arran in the hand.

"Damn it, man!" Arran snapped. He squeezed his hand to determine how badly he was cut. Blood welled along the line and dripped sluggishly across his palm.

It would not need stitching. Which was good because Kieran had lost hold of his temper and could have done real damage to Arran without meaning to.

"I'm sorry. I am not sure why I am in such a foul mood today." He shook his head and ran a hand through his hair. "There's nothing wrong with Ellie—Ella. Nothing at all." He looked up at the blue sky and the few puffy clouds crossing above them. "In truth, she is perfect. Much too good for you. Or me for that matter."

Arran raised his brow. "I thought you were promised."

"I am."

"Are ye certain?"

"I have to be. I have no other choice."

Arran nodded. "I see."

And Kieran thought the man did see. He must have seen more than Kieran did.

"I would not make a bad husband," Arran assured him.

Kieran was not the person Arran would need to get permission from in order to court Ella. Teague would measure Arran and make such a decision. But where Teague might actually consider the man a good choice, Kieran wouldn't give up so easily.

"She didn't come here looking for a husband. She came her to see to her aunt."

"And her aunt seems to be well enough. Perhaps she would like to come to the castle for the meal as well. They would both be welcome as my guests."

"Ellie doesn't have any fancy dresses here. You would only embarrass her."

Kieran felt his face warm with shame for his desperate attempts to keep Arran away from her.

"One of my warrior's sisters is her size. I can see that she's provided a proper gown for the meal. I think mayhap both women would enjoy a meal they didn't have to make themselves. As well as entertainment."

Kieran couldn't argue—Arran seemed to have thought of everything.

"Very well," Kieran said and then set to thrashing the man again.

After a dip in the loch to wash away the sweat of his efforts, Kieran went to the cottage to extend Arran's invitation that the ladies come to the castle for the late meal. He felt like an awkward messenger boy, delivering their excited reply back to Arran so he could have a dress sent for Ellie.

Kieran had planned to escort the women from the village to the castle, but Arran arrived just in time and offered Ellie his arm.

Kieran did the same for Jenny, who chuckled at his glum expression.

"You seem to be in a mood this evening. Has something happened?" Jenny asked him while gripping his arm as if she feared he would run away and leave her stranded to walk up to the castle alone. As if the woman couldn't walk that far on her own. She was not some withered old woman.

"I'm fine."

"Ella said the two of you plan to leave tomorrow?"

"Aye. Now that we've seen to your health, I should return."

"But she's only just gotten here, and she seems to be having an enjoyable visit. Mayhap she could stay with me and someone could see her home in a week or so."

"Nay. I gave her father my word I would see her safely home. I'll not shirk my duties onto someone else."

"I wouldn't see it as shirking your duty. I could easily write to my brother and tell him I wished for Ella's company."

"When did everyone start calling her Ella? She's always been Ellie to me, but now it seems she doesn't like it. I fear I missed her telling me, or mayhap she didn't tell me. Maybe I should have noticed everyone else called her Ella. Even her father calls her Ella, now that I think about it. How absurd."

It was not at all what they were talking about, but Kieran had wondered on it all day and could no longer keep it bottled up inside.

When Kieran looked over at Jenny, she offered him a knowing smile.

"My apologies. I didn't mean to change the subject so abruptly." He struggled to remember what they had been discussing.

The woman had suggested Ella stay behind with her—and Arran—while he returned to Girnigoe alone. No, that wouldn't do. But he didn't have a good reason why.

Generally, when one didn't have a good argument, they simply stated their original argument in another way.

"I cannot just abandon her. She is my responsibility. For a little while longer at least."

"And when she ceases being your responsibility, she might return?" Jenny blinked innocently up at him.

Kieran wished to talk about anything else. He picked up their pace when he realized Ella and Arran were getting some distance ahead.

"If she wishes," he practically snapped at her.

"Then doesn't it make sense that we should just ask her now if she wishes to stay, to avoid all that extra travel for no reason?"

"I imagine so."

"Very well. We will ask her later this evening what she wishes to do. Stay here or go."

The way she put it made it clear it wasn't a decision about staying or leaving, but something more complicated. Ella would be choosing him or Arran. And she couldn't pick him. He wasn't available.

Giving up, Kieran could only nod. He feared if he spoke, he might attempt to win this debate in some other ridiculous way. And the woman was right. It was Ella's decision whether she stayed or not. And more importantly, who she would choose.

Who was he to think he could order her about? It had never worked for him in the past; she'd just get mule-headed and insist on having her way.

Mayhap he should have mentioned that trait to Arran when he'd asked about Ella. Would her stubbornness keep the man at bay?

From the way Arran was staring at Ella as they walked ahead of them, it seemed not.

"You've spent some time with the man. Do you know of any reason why he is unsuitable for Ella?" Jenny asked.

He considered the question, wanting to bestow a list of the man's shortcomings, but he let out a breath and shook his head.

"Not a one. He's honorable and has income to support a wife and a family."

"He treats her with respect," Jenny said, nodding to the couple in front of them.

"Aye."

"That is all a friend could ask for another *friend*, is it not?" Damn but the woman was picking at all his wounds this night.

Kieran looked at Ella's aunt, who seemed to see right through him to the monster within.

"I want her to be happy, I do. I just . . ."

"Just what? Want her to be happy with you?"

Yes! "Nay," he answered. "I just don't want her to leave Caithness."

"You don't want her to leave you."

"Aye," Kieran admitted quietly. "Yes. I think that is what I'm struggling with. That if she marries, she will leave and I'll not see her any longer."

"Do you think that fate is worse than to be cast aside while her best friend marries another and goes about his duties, leaving her behind?"

"I don't want that for her. I had hoped that wouldn't

happen."

He and Ella had held out hope that Kieran's new wife would accept their friendship, perhaps even join their group. But even if that happened, it would not be like it was now.

"I want her to be happy," Kieran said simply. Even more fortunate was that he meant it. He'd thought he'd completely given over to becoming a selfish arse, but it seemed under all his fear he was still Ella's friend at heart.

"She looks to be happy at the moment." Jenny nodded to the two people laughing ahead of them.

"Then I will be happy for them as well." And damn if he wouldn't work to make that happen. Even if he felt miserable at the moment.

"Trust me, for I know well about this. The worst thing you could do to someone you care for is to sentence them to having to watch someone they love leave them behind."

"Aye. I'll do my best not to be a selfish clod-head."

"Ye do that."

Chapter Thirteen

Ella looked back at Kieran as she entered the hall on Arran's arm. She was often nervous when meeting new people or being the center of attention. She rather wished Kieran had walked beside her so he could tell her all was well.

"Is everything all right?" Arran asked when she stopped in the hall. "Besides the fact that everyone appears to be looking at you." He laughed and then patted her hand where it rested on his arm.

It should have been reassuring. It was reassuring. Just not as reassuring as if Kieran had done it.

This time when she looked back at Kieran, he winked

and gave her a nod. And despite him being a few feet behind her, she calmed.

"I believe we should present you at the high table first," Arran suggested.

Ella nodded in agreement.

"My laird," Arran said loudly. "I'm sure you remember your niece Ellisay Ross."

"Ah, yes, Ella, you have grown since last I saw you."

Ella bowed and nodded. "Aye, my laird," she said, though she had been there just last year and hadn't changed much since then. But her uncle would be too busy being laird to remember anything about her.

"Brother," Jenny said, and Ella thought she sounded rather peevish. Ella pressed her lips together so as not to smile.

"Sister. I understand you were ill recently. I had not known."

"It was nothing for you to be concerned over, *laird*." Yes, Jenny was definitely displeased with her oldest brother.

"We missed you at the games."

"I was so sorry I was unable to attend."

As lies went, Jenny and her brother were terrible at them. Mayhap that was on purpose.

"Of course, you will sit at the high table in a place of honor," the laird said, and Ella did her best not to frown. A place of honor meant being front and center for all to see and gawk at.

Arran sat at the laird's right hand. Ella sat next to him with Kieran to her right and Jenny at the end of the table.

"Pay no attention to the rest of the hall. They are surely looking at me, not you," Kieran said, causing her to laugh. If anyone would have heard him, they would have thought him vain for such a remark. Only Ella knew he said it in jest.

"If I do something to embarrass myself, you must do something even worse to draw everyone's attention from me," she said.

"Aye. I'll be ready."

She nudged his ribs with her elbow, but he only looked down at her with a grin.

"I still plan to return to Girnigoe in the morning. Your aunt thinks you will wish to stay here longer. It is up to ye." Kieran spoke the words casually. Only someone who knew him so well would have noticed the underlying tension in his face.

He meant what he said—that it was up to her. But he wanted her to go with him. Nay, he wanted her to choose him.

Before she had a chance to answer, or think of how to answer, one of the serving maids came forward to fill Kieran's tankard with ale. Ella couldn't help but notice the way the woman leaned over him so her ample breasts were nearly right in his face. If that didn't make the woman's intensions clear, her lusty smile and wink sure did.

"I'll see you don't go without something you need, my laird."

"He's not a laird," Ella snapped.

"Aye. But he'll be so one day," the woman said before moving on.

Another woman brought their meals, and while this one wasn't as obvious, she still stood much too close for the task of serving food. Ella would know; she helped in the hall at Girnigoe. It gave her something to do. And a reason to be at the castle.

She had never needed to lean so close to someone to deliver a trencher of haggis.

"Is something the matter?" Arran asked, drawing her attention away from Kieran and his line of ample maids to deliver his every desire.

"The maids here are quite bold." In truth, they were probably no less bold than the maids at Girnigoe. It was only that here, Kieran was a new toy to play with, so all attentions seemed to be focused on him.

Arran smiled. "Only with honored guests. Especially ones that will be laird someday."

"He's to be wed. They have no chance with him."
Their chance had not been good even before he was betrothed,

but now it was nil.

"They may have no chance to wed him, but he's not married yet."

"Kieran would never entertain such women."

Arran appeared surprised. "He speaks to ye of such things?"

Ella realized she shouldn't have noticed or spoken of any of this. And, in truth, Kieran hadn't exactly spoken to her on this topic, regardless of how many times she'd asked him.

Rather than answer, she simply shrugged and turned to Kieran.

"Do ye plan to spend the night with one of these women?" Ella asked him.

His brows came together in confusion before he asked, "What women?"

She laughed at his attempt to feign ignorance. He winked, and her breath caught.

Arran had winked at her on at least two occasions as they traversed up to the castle from Jenny's cottage, and neither time had she reacted as she did when Kieran winked at her.

Perhaps it was just a matter of comfort. If she were able to get to know Arran better, mayhap his winks would make her breath catch as well.

If she left in the morning with Kieran, she wouldn't

have an opportunity to get to know Arran better. But to stay meant she would miss out on the short time she and Kieran had left together before everything changed. There would be time after Kieran wed for her to come back to Kildary and spend time with Arran.

Mind made up, she leaned closer to Kieran.

"I'll be ready to leave with you in the morning."

*

Kieran didn't sleep well. He thought he was eager to be home, but as he dressed and went to get the horses tacked, he realized he was eager to leave Kildary with Ella, and for their travels home more than arriving at home.

He was also dealing with a fair bit of guilt.

He'd wanted her to choose him. But when she had, he realized he'd been wrong to want that. It was a selfish thing no friend should have done.

To want her for himself when he could not give her anything in return.

And worse was knowing he should bid her to stay so she'd have the opportunity to know Arran, but he was unable to speak the words.

He was not a good friend. He was a monster.

The cottage door opened, but instead of Ella, it was

Jenny who came out. Kieran had a moment of unease that perhaps Ella had changed her mind until he saw the scowl on Jenny's face.

It was the same as it had been last night when Ella had announced she would be returning home with him.

"I did not think you selfish like your father, Kieran Sinclair."

Kieran didn't care for being likened to his father. Rolfe was respected and well-liked by the clan as well as the neighboring clans, but on a personal level, Kieran hoped not to ever be like him. If he was one day blessed with children, he would not treat them as his father had treated him.

"Am I to leave her here? Just run off and abandon her? She said she wanted to leave. I didn't make her." Kieran's response was rather snappish, and he realized he was angry with Jenny because she made him feel even more guilty over what he'd done.

"You shouldn't have asked. You must know how the lass feels about ye. Do you wish to hurt her in this way?"

"Of course not. And we are friends. We have always been, and I hope to God we will be able to remain so after I'm wed. I don't want to lose her friendship."

Jenny shook her head and waved a hand at him.

"Ye Sinclairs. Ye do what you want without any regard to others and what is best for them."

Kieran wanted to lash back at her, wanted to know what right she had to compare him to his father when she didn't know him. But it didn't matter, for Jenny turned sharply and went back inside, letting him stand there holding their horses.

"Am I being selfish, Ridire?" he whispered to his horse, who snorted and shook his head. "Thank ye, lad. I've packed an apple for you." He patted his loyal mount.

When the door opened this time, Ella came out with a smile.

"I don't know what you did to Aunt Jenny, but you've put her in a mood."

"She doesn't care for me," Kieran said honestly. At the moment, he couldn't say he blamed her, but with Ella smiling at him the way she was, it stripped away any strength he might need to do the right thing.

Ella waved her hand. "Are we ready?"

"Did you pack us some of those tarts you made?"

She answered with an annoyed, "Pfft. Of course. But they are for later."

He helped her mount, taking note of how slim her waist was and how his fingers fit perfectly along her ribs. He mounted his own horse, being careful of the predicament under his kilt caused by touching her.

He reined his horse to the side, but Ella stopped him

by digging in her bag and handing him a tart.

"It's later."

He laughed and shook his head. "Ye spoil me, Ella."

"You've always needed a bit of spoiling," she said, causing him to grow harder still. Even knowing she hadn't meant it that way. But all he could think about was how she might spoil him with her lips and body against his.

Kieran managed to shake off the foolish thoughts as they rode out of the village. He watched her as they crested the hill, where the castle would no longer be visible. When Kildary and everyone there would be out of sight. Would Ella look back?

He realized he was hoping she wouldn't, for if she gave him the barest idea she didn't wish to go, he would turn them back and tell her to stay.

She didn't look back. She didn't look anything other than happy to be riding next to him.

Jenny had been wrong. He wasn't being selfish by asking her to come with him. This was truly where she wanted to be. Anyone could see that.

But an hour into their travels, she began talking about Arran and didn't stop until Kieran could not take any more and ordered them to stop to water the horses.

He left her to her necessities so he could walk the horses into a shallow stream for them to drink. Ridire snorted.

"Aye, laddie, I'm happy for the silence as well." He stood there in the river longer than needed, just giving himself a moment to calm down.

But as he returned to her, any calm he had managed to scrape together was undone when the first thing out of her mouth was, "I wonder if this is the stream Arran mentioned. He said—"

"Good God, woman. How could he have said so much in the short time you spent with the man? If ye are so caught up by him, why did you leave with me?" He was near to shouting, which was something he'd never done to Ella. It was no wonder she just stood there in shock for a moment.

But when she managed to shake off her surprise, she let him have it.

"I left with ye because you asked me to," she said.

"Nay. I only asked if you wanted to come home now or if you wished to come home later. It was your choice to make."

"And we both know I wasn't making a choice about when I wished to return home, didn't we?"

"I don't understand you. What other choice was there to make?" Though, of course, he knew what she meant.

She stepped closer so she could point her finger into his chest. The gold in her brown eyes blazed as she yelled at him.

"You wanted me to go with you. You wanted me to pick you!"

It was as if she'd broken some rule in speaking something that wasn't meant to be spoken, and at such an impressive volume.

"Aye! I did want you to pick me!" he said, feeling as if he might fall over for how sharply his world had tilted. Was he going daft? But a moment later, the question of his daftness was answered when he bent down and kissed her.

Chapter Fourteen

Ella stood still for two breaths while she contemplated how this had happened. One moment they were screaming at each other loud enough to make the horses shy, and the next he was kissing her.

Not just kissing her, but claiming her completely.

And damn if she didn't want to be claimed by Kieran Sinclair.

She opened to him, allowing his tongue to slide into her mouth and tangle with hers. That was different from when last they'd kissed. No, everything about this was different than the last time. As different as sunrise and sunset. Summer and winter.

His body was larger than he'd been back then. Of course, she'd known he'd grown into a large man, but she'd not realized quite how much space he took up until it was her space he was taking.

She reached up, her hands tangling in his longish black hair. His large hands spanned her waist, much as they did when he'd hoisted her into her saddle, but that was different as well. His hands were higher on her ribs, his thumbs stroked just under her breasts, and she wanted to move them higher so they could touch her where she needed him.

Instead, his hands slid down her back until they were over her arse, and then he squeezed and pulled her closer to his body. She felt the hardness of him where his kilt was tented away from his legs.

The place between her legs throbbed for him, and she moaned without knowing she was capable of such a wanton sound.

Kieran fairly growled in response, and his lips moved from hers to catch her under her jaw and down her neck. She'd never known she could feel these things. She'd never known that spot on her neck was connected to other parts on her body—parts of her body that seemed to just now come to life. Her breasts ached for attention, and she worried she would catch on fire, but the only word she could utter was, "Yes."

But this word seemed to have the opposite effect on Kieran. For he pulled away and stared at her, blinking rapidly. It was as if he only just realized who he had been kissing. Or mayhap a demon had possessed him and left his body abruptly.

"I—I'm sorry, Ella. Forgive me." He didn't give her a chance to say anything in response, he just rushed off into the trees, leaving her standing there with their horses.

With shaky hands, she reached up to touch her lips where they fairly tingled from his kiss. They felt swollen, but with no pain.

It had been a wonderful kiss. It was everything she had dreamed of when she'd dreamed of him in her bed at home. Her body reacted in much the same way as it had when she'd woken frustrated and needy.

Except he was here. Or rather he had been a moment ago.

Knowing Kieran as well as she did, it was no surprise he had run from her after he'd returned to himself. He would never want to hurt her or take advantage of their friendship.

But his running away stung, and the longer it took for him to return, the more irritated she became.

He was ruining this perfect moment. A moment that seemed inevitable. Something had been growing between them since the day he'd told her he was to marry. Some fog had been lifted and the sun had shone directly on their friendship.

Without the shadows of their youth, the truth had been exposed openly.

They were friends, yes, but there was something else there.

Something wonderful.

Something they couldn't keep.

Her breath caught and she tried to swallow when that bigger piece of the truth fell into place.

*

What had he done? Kieran asked himself the question for the sixth time as he trudged along the creek. It wouldn't do for him to get himself lost in the forest. Even as much as he might want to.

He would have to go back. He shouldn't have left her alone even for a moment. Teague would not be pleased for his poor escort.

Of course, Teague would not be pleased to know how Kieran had disrespected his daughter.

He let a list of curses fly in English as well as Gaelic. Some Ella had taught him.

This was exactly what he'd known could not happen. As much as he'd enjoyed it and would hold the memory of her kiss for the rest of his life, it was wrong of him to take it.

Not when he couldn't give her everything she deserved.

This was the worst thing a friend could do. But it was now clear he was no kind of a friend. That knowledge hurt the most. To think he had failed in this as well.

Eventually, he gave up on berating himself and turned to go back.

He didn't know what he would say. Ella would no doubt want to discuss it so it wasn't stuck between them, but he would have to decline. It was too raw.

What was worse was knowing as bad as he felt about hurting Ella, the monster inside him wanted to kiss her again.

"That can't happen," he whispered to himself as he walked back into the clearing. "Are we ready to get on our way again?" His question was spoken casually with a voice that sounded steadier than he felt.

Inside, he was shaken and panicked.

"I was only waiting for you to return from your little fit," she said to rile him. He ignored her and went to stand next to her horse.

Rather than risk touching her, he laced his fingers and held them out, ready to take her boot and give her a boost up into her saddle.

With a sigh, she gave him a shove.

"I don't need your help. Go away."

She was angry at him. This was good. Angry people didn't kiss one another.

Except that was exactly what had happened earlier. They'd been sparring one moment, and he'd reached for her the next. Apparently, the passion that came from arguing was not so different from other kinds of passion.

He would need to be careful in the future.

They rode on in silence for more than hour. Kieran thought perhaps the event would be forgotten, and eventually they could go back to how things had been.

But, of course, he should have known better. Ella was not one to just let something fade away without discussing it.

"Should we talk about what happened?" she asked.

"Nay. I beg of you, Ella, let us never speak of it." He feared *never* would be too soon.

"Then it will be this awkwardness between us forever?"

"'Tis not awkward. 'Tis just too soon. It will be better. With time we will forget." He wouldn't forget. Not as long as he lived.

"And if I don't wish to forget it because it was wonderful?"

Christ, the woman was set on killing him. Despite his distress, he did feel his heart warm to know she'd thought their kiss wonderful. He'd felt the same. Mayhap *wonderful* was not a large enough word to describe how incredible their kiss had been.

So different from when they'd kissed when they were younger. It was not just a touch of lips this time. It was a claiming. He'd claimed her, but she'd claimed him right back.

"You may do what you wish. I just ask you to leave me to deal with it how I wish." Which was apparently to be cross with her while torturing himself with the memories of how sweet her lips had been with the hint of blackberry jam left from the tarts they'd had earlier.

Would he ever be able to eat a blackberry tart again without thinking of her mouth on his? Her tongue tangled with his? Damn, but he was hard again.

"And you wish to forget it?" Her words were no longer tinged with anger. He could hear the hurt he had caused.

He had no choice but to offer her honesty. They had been friends their whole lives, and to lie to her now about something so important would be a betrayal of all the time between them.

"I don't want to forget it. I'll never be able to forget it. I will treasure the memory of it as I live my life with the bride that was chosen for me. And God help me, but I will likely think of it when I'm with her. It's wrong, I know, but I have never felt something as that kiss, Ella. And doubt I will again."

A rumble of thunder interrupted whatever she might have said.

"Come, we must find shelter before this storm hits," he ordered as if he hadn't just professed how he felt.

The words had come unbidden, but they were the truth he'd hidden all this time from her. Hidden from himself as well.

Chapter Fifteen

Kieran led them to a place in the hills as if he knew the way. Rocks set out from a hill in staggered tiers slanted down. He settled the horses under the lowest outcropping and removed their tack, tucking it deeper under the lower end to keep dry. Ella watched him as if he was a different person.

She noticed how strong and capable he was as the muscles along his back bunched and moved under his shirt.

"Have you been here before?" she asked.

"Aye. 'Tis called Hill House, for the rocks look like roofs." He assisted her up the steep incline to the next level and probably the deepest recess. The walls were marked with soot from previous fires. He set her bedroll off to one side of the area and carried his own to the farthest side away from her.

She wasn't sure if he didn't trust her or himself. Mayhap both of them were in danger from the other. It seemed they both wanted something, and with that silent agreement, it meant no one would be capable of reason when called upon.

"Since we are not wet, we don't need a fire. Let us just sleep and be on our way at first light so we can get home," he said with more than a hint of frustration.

For the first time since she had decided to return home with him, she wondered if she'd made the right choice. If she'd stayed behind, they would not be in this situation.

"You are angry," she said. He hadn't raised his voice since his heated admission, but he was not his smiling self either.

"I-I'm angry with myself, Ella. Not with you," he admitted. His shoulders fell as if all the fight had drained out of him.

He was never angry with her, despite all the things she'd done that should have angered him as children. He was ever patient and kind. It was as comforting as it was irritating.

"We did nothing wrong," she said. "You are not yet wed. You've taken no vows."

"I know that. And since she is a stranger, I owe her nothing more until I take those vows, but it's still wrong of me to put us in a position to want things we canna have."

She nodded. She understood and was grateful. Or wanted to be. But part of her only saw what she could have and what she wanted. And what she might regret if they didn't use their time together to the fullest.

The rain started in earnest, tapping on the stone edge not covered by the rocks above it. They were safe and dry where they were.

The storm took the last of the light, and soon she was lying on her furs in complete darkness as the storm raged outside their shelter. It may not have been cold enough for a fire, but the damp air and the cool rock under her caused a chill. She wished to be able to curl up next to Kieran as she had on their way to Kildary.

But everything had changed. If they were that close now, one of them would surely give in and kiss the other. Most likely her. Of the two of them, she was the weaker in this.

Strange, since she'd always thought it was men who could not resist their base urges. She recalled the women in the hall serving the men with an inviting smile. Perhaps the truth of the matter was that men were better able to resist such pleasure than women were.

Well, she would not make a fool of herself again. She remained on her fur the whole night and must have fallen asleep at some point, for she woke to a bright, sunny morning and Kieran gathering up his things.

He'd said he wanted to leave at first light, but it was later as the sun was fully in the sky. The storm had left behind an earthy scent in the forest.

"I'll help you down," Kieran said in the same stiff voice he'd used the night before. He took her arm only long enough for her to land on the ground next to him before he stepped back and pointed. "There is a small stream in that direction."

She opened her mouth to say something but closed it when the right words did not come.

As she took care of necessities and washed, she wondered if mayhap this wasn't better. To allow this distance to grow between them. It might make it easier later when they could no longer spend time together. She'd originally thought it best to use the most of their time, but perhaps it was best to prepare for the inevitable end of them.

Ella hated crying, but she allowed a few tears to fall before she went back to the horses and to the man she was not ready to let go of.

*

All night Kieran had wanted to go to her, or for Ella to come to him, but neither had acted. He'd thought it for the best, but now, as they rode for home, he didn't like how things had been left.

Eventually, he could stand it no longer and he stopped his horse.

To allow them to go on as they were would mean the end of their friendship. He could see that now. Knew where this destructive silence would lead.

Ella stopped a distance away. She'd been next to him earlier but had drifted behind at some point. He felt as if he was losing her already.

"What is it?" she asked when he got down from his horse and came back to her.

"Get down." He reached for her before she had a chance to argue, and with a flick of the reins both horses were hobbled so they could graze in the field next to the forest.

"Are you hungry?" she asked. "Because I've no tarts left."

"Nay, I'm not hungry," he said but then reconsidered the question. "Yes. I am hungry. But not for food."

She gave him a befuddled look as he came closer. But rather than step back as she should have, she stepped closer. A move that secured their fate.

They seemed to reach for each other at the same time, his hands framing her face as her arms came around him, holding him close.

He bent toward her, but it was she who reached up to kiss him first.

Once they were kissing, it was as if a fire had been lit, burning everything touched by the flames.

"Ella . . . Ella . . ." He could only manage to say her name as he kissed her. Her lips, the edge of her jaw, her throat and neck, the flesh of her heaving chest.

She pulled away, and when she went toward her horse, he worried he'd stepped too far. Would she leave him?

But she simply reached up to pull down a plaid from her saddle and then, folding it over her arm, she held her hand out in invitation.

"Come, let us find a quiet place."

He followed her into the coolness of the forest. She glanced around, but he knew what she was looking for.

"Here." He pointed to a grassy place where the sun reached through the trees to warm the earth.

She nodded and set out the plaid before dropping to the blanket to remove her boots. He did the same and sank to his knees beside her. It seemed they were both of the same mind about what they wanted and what was to happen now, but even so, he would have her approval before just assuming as much.

"Ella. I want you. It is wrong for I canna offer you marriage after. If you don't want this, I would understand."

"I want this too, Kieran. And I know our future will not see us together, but I want this memory with you. If I never find a husband of my own, I want to have this time to look back and remember."

He nodded and then recalled another truth he needed to share with her.

"I've not lain with anyone," he admitted.

She raised a brow, and he smiled.

"I didn't lie. Not really. I allowed you to assume, and I didn't correct ye."

She smiled and nodded.

"I am glad. This will just be for us."

He understood what she meant, but he shook his head.

"I agree that this step will be better for us taking it together, but it would have maybe been an easier step if one of us knew our way."

"Animals don't need anyone to tell them how it's done. We'll find our own way, Kieran. I'm sure of it."

He nodded and reached to pull his shirt over his head.

Teague had offered to see to the matter of Kieran's virginity when he'd been ten and six. Kieran hadn't wanted to lie with a woman he didn't know. He blamed his friendship with a lass as the reason he could not take pleasure from a woman for coin. It seemed disrespectful and wrong. Ella had always made the act sound sacred. And while he'd been eager to find his way, he didn't want to go about it so carelessly.

"Besides," she said as she rolled off her stockings. "We do know how one goes about it. We saw the stable master with the maid that time."

"Aye. I've seen it a few other times as well, and there's the fact that men talk about it all the time." It seemed all the men talked about. The act of swiving, who they'd swived, and who they wanted to swive.

Kieran had a formidable education, if no personal experience.

But that was about to change. And while he was a bit nervous about it, he wasn't worried, for it was Ella. They had shared everything with each other. It only made sense they would share this as well.

Feeling heartened by that knowledge, he reached for her and bent to kiss her as he'd wanted to do since the last time their lips had touched.

His body responded, but this time he didn't need to hide his cockstand from her. She was about to see him in all his glory. And he would see her.

"We seem very good at kissing," Ella said. "It's reasonable to think we shall be good at the rest of it."

He smiled against her lips.

"Aye. Let us find out."

*

Ella feared her heart might beat right out of her body for as fast as it was going. Her breathing had picked up, quicker than ever before. It was as if she'd run a great distance, yet she hadn't moved at all. If she were going to die, she hoped it would happen after she and Kieran had this moment. But people didn't die from the act. She knew that much at least.

She was still pressed up against Kieran's chest with his arms holding her tightly to him. As if he worried she might try to escape.

That was not likely. There was nowhere she wanted to be but here with him.

Something felt odd about her gown, and she realized he'd loosened it. She wanted to commend him on his ability to disrobe her while also kissing her neck and bosom, but she was too distracted by the feeling of his warm tongue on her nipple to speak at all.

Kieran should not have worried they wouldn't know what to do. They were already off to a delicious start.

Ella worked at the buckle on Kieran's weapons belt and nearly shouted for joy when it finally freed and fell to the ground. She next ran her hands over his bare chest and stomach. She'd seen him many times without a shirt, but she'd never had the opportunity to touch him.

She was surprised when she ran her finger over his flat nipple that the touch caused a moan from Kieran. Mayhap men's nipples were as sensitive as a woman's. She hadn't known.

She had to wait before moving onto the belt that held his kilt when he took over and stripped her gown off her body. She felt exposed standing in the middle of the forest in just her shift, but before she could think more on it, her shift was pulled over her head as well.

She looked down at her bare skin and back to him, watching as his gaze traveled over her. She need not worry he was displeased with her body, for he was muttering his praise almost like a prayer.

"Good heavens, Ella, ye are so beautiful. I don't know what I want to touch first."

Kieran kneeled on the plaid and placed soft kisses to her breasts, sucking and licking her nipples. He moved along her ribs as his large hands cupped her arse. Squeezing and holding her in place, he kissed lower still. When his lips touched the place where her body and her legs met, an intense tingle went through her body, making it difficult to remain standing. Fortunately, Kieran must have noticed, for he gently tugged her down onto the blanket to lie next to him.

They kissed again and continued kissing until she was practically begging for more of him. And then he touched her in the place that needed him most.

"Wet," he whispered, and for a moment she wondered what he meant until he moved his fingers and she felt the way they moved easily where she was slick with desire for him.

It wasn't the first time he'd managed to make her respond in this way, but it was so much better when he touched her there. And then his finger slipped inside her body, and it was somehow even better.

"Kieran," she said but didn't know what else she meant to say. It was as if her mind was in some fog of lust. She couldn't think. There was nothing else in the world except the two of them and the way Kieran was touching her.

When Kieran slipped a second finger into her, she felt her first twinge of concern. She knew the first time a woman lay with a man there was some pain involved as her maidenhead was penetrated. She'd overheard the maids speaking of it once as if it was no more than a bother. Ella thought pain in any way was to be avoided, and she worried about Kieran's size.

He was large. Tall and broad. It only made sense that the part of him under his kilt would be large as well. His fingers seemed to stretch her there; his member would do far worse.

"What is it?" he asked.

"Nothing," she said. She didn't want him to think her a

ninny to be worried over a bit of pain. She'd spent most of her life proving she was as brave as any man. As brave as Kieran. But in this, she didn't feel quite as brave.

What if she screamed from the pain? She knew Kieran well enough to know he'd feel guilty over it.

He paused in kissing her, and after removing his fingers from her body, he raised his hand, the one with the scar. Before he spoke, she knew what he would say.

"We promised to only speak the truth to one another."

She swallowed and nodded. "I'm a bit worried over the pain part of it."

"I'm a bit worried over that part as well," he confided while resting his forehead against hers. "Do you wish to stop?"

"Nay," she said quickly.

He let out a breath and shook his head.

"Ella, this isn't about proving anything to me or anyone else. If you don't want to do this. If you're scared—"

"I'm not scared," she argued. "I said I was a bit worried, not scared."

"Of course, I didn't mean to say you were scared. I know well enough you see it as a challenge when you're accused of being frightened of something, but this is different. And I am scared. I'm not afraid to tell you the truth."

"Do you want to stop?" she asked, not sure how she wanted him to answer.

He let out a breath and then shook his head.

"I want this with you more than I've wanted anything, so no, I don't want to stop. But I'm not the one who will be hurt, and I'll not push you if you don't want to do this."

She let out a breath and kissed him again. Once more, heat flamed between them, and soon she was as needy as before. Mayhap even worse. She couldn't imagine having to stop with this empty feeling gnawing at her forever.

"I don't wish to stop, but let's get on with it so we can get past that part. I have heard it is much better afterward."

"Very well." He backed away and knelt before her so he could remove the belt holding his kilt. When the fabric dropped away, she stared at the beast pointing out at her.

She'd seen Kieran naked before. Once when they were younger and he was swimming in the loch, she'd come upon him when he was getting out of the water. She thought it would have grown over the years, and having felt it pressed against her recently, she knew it was large.

But she hadn't been prepared for this.

She lay back and closed her eyes.

"Hurry, Kieran."

He chuckled, and when she opened her eyes, he was shaking his head.

"I don't wish to hurry," he said as his smile faded and he looked at her with warmth and passion in his gaze. "I want us to remember this moment forever and how wonderful it was."

She nodded but wasn't sure how wonderful it might be.

He lowered himself over her, keeping his weight from her body with his arms, while she allowed her legs to open, inviting him closer.

He kissed her again, and she welcomed the comforting haze that had her clutching his shoulders and pulling him closer. Her body wanted this despite her distress. She decided to listen to her body.

"Please, Kieran," she begged. He moaned when she felt the heat of him in the place his fingers had been. He moved around a bit, and for a moment she thought she might be different from other women because it felt so glorious with him inside her—there was no pain at all.

But then he pushed farther and farther still, and there was a bit of stretching and burning, but it was not so much to pull her completely from her fog of pleasure, and then with a quick jolt the worst was over, and he waited, watching her.

"Are you all right, Ella?"

"I am now. It was not so bad, really."

He breathed out a sigh of what she knew was relief before he kissed her again. He moved, out and back in, and each time he did so, the pain eased even more until it was completely gone.

In its place came a different feeling. Something she hadn't felt before. Pleasure building upon itself, growing bigger and more vehement with each thrust.

She called his name as she went over, not sure if she wanted him to save her or thank him.

She'd heard it was much better after the pain, but she hadn't known it would be the most amazing thing she'd ever experienced.

Would ever experience.

Chapter Sixteen

Kieran had kissed a few lasses in his time, had touched a few as well, but nothing lit his heart on fire like holding on to Ella and kissing her, loving her.

He could feel his body pushing to thrust into her harder and take his release, but only when he felt her body pulsing around his did he give in.

Remembering at the last moment what he'd been told about spending his seed in a woman, he pulled from Ella's body, despite his desire to let go deeper inside her, as was natural.

Spending on the blanket next to them seemed wrong.

But it was the best he could do to protect her, and he would always protect Ella.

For all his strength, he was suddenly weak and slumped next to her, his head resting on her chest, where he could hear the hammering of her heart.

He was sure his own heart raced in the same way. He'd never felt anything so wonderful. He'd seen to his own pleasure countless times, but it was so different with a warm woman. The way she moved, the sounds she made. The way she smelled.

He finally understood why the warriors spent most of their time talking of it.

As their bodies calmed, she reached up and ran her fingers through his hair. It was nearly as wonderful being held and caressed as it was being inside her.

Maybe not, but at this moment when he could barely move, he was happy to just lie there with the sun warming his bare back as she touched him.

But as their hearts slowed and their breathing returned to normal, he began to wonder what would happen next.

They always made plans. They knew when and where they would meet when they set out on an adventure. This was new and unexpected.

But mayhap it shouldn't have been such a surprise. All their lives seemed to lead them to this moment. Whatever this moment turned out to be.

Except he knew what it could never be. It couldn't be their future.

In a few months, he would marry another, and once he gave his word to be faithful to his wife, he would be. No matter how much he wanted Ella.

They couldn't be together.

*

Ella and Kieran had never been so close before. They had rarely touched, and never like this. Casual brushes of their fingers as they passed things back and forth. Occasional touches when they shared a bench or log and their hips would meet for a moment until they adjusted.

"I can't think of the last time anyone has touched me," he said as if he'd heard her thoughts. He liked to tease her when she seemed to read his mind, but if she was a witch, he was able to do the same kind of magic himself.

She considered his words while her fingers continued to brush through his soft black hair.

"I guess I take such things for granted. My da has always given me hugs or patted my head affectionately."

"I like this," he said, settling against her.

She liked it as well, but she imagined it was different

for him, being starved for any kind of affection from a father who seemed incapable of loving this dear person.

"I'm sorry your father treats you the way he does." How many times had she said those words over the years?

She wished she could hate the laird for the pain he'd caused his son, but deep down she knew the older man acted out of his own pain. It didn't make it right. But it made Ella hurt for them both. For the way they might have been able to heal one another if only they could see past their heartache and fear.

Kieran shrugged off her concern, but she didn't let it go. Her friend saw himself as lacking, and she never wanted him to believe it. It wasn't true.

"For all it isn't right, you might even be better off for it. For you've become a fine man, Kier. A good man. A kind man."

He raised his head and looked at her. The silence between them grew, their eyes locked on each other.

Once again, she struggled to breathe normally.

And then in a movement as natural as the blink of an eye, he leaned forward and pressed his lips to hers.

Their dance began anew, but he rolled to pull her on top of him.

For a moment, she wondered why he would do such a thing, but when she felt his cock lurch under her in the place where they would join, she realized it would be easy enough to rise up enough to settle back down with him inside of her.

She did just that, thinking she was quite clever, but then she realized she probably hadn't been the first to discover such a thing could work between bodies.

And then she didn't care, for they were moving together again. It felt different this time, with no worry over pain or the unknown.

She knew exactly what could happen, that rush of pleasure and bliss, and waited for it.

"You feel so good," he said as he pushed up from beneath her. She might have argued that she couldn't feel as good as he felt to her but decided now was not the time for them to get into a heated argument about something that couldn't be proven.

She just kept moving until that rush came. Kieran sat up and thrust into her a few more times before lifting her and turning away as his release came.

She knew why he didn't spend his seed inside of her, for it could get her with child.

She felt a flare of anger, knowing they would never have a child together. Kieran was destined to father children with his wife.

And she would be alone.

Unless she married someone else.

As her blood cooled, she thought of Arran. Trying to imagine the two of them doing what she had done with Kieran. Her mind was unable to produce such a thought. Not now, with Kieran's clean, earthy scent surrounding her and his warm body under hers where she'd collapsed.

His large hands traced up and down her back, claiming the touch he hadn't been permitted.

They lay there until the sun started to lower in the sky.

"I don't think we shall make it back to Caithness today," she said.

"Were you in a hurry to return home?" he asked with a knowing grin.

"Nay. I'm in no hurry."

His grin faded. "I wish time would stop and we could just stay here like this. Then I wouldn't . . ."

Letting out a breath, he shook his head.

"Let us not think of what will come. Let us have this time for just us."

She nodded in agreement as her stomach growled.

"Aye," he said, kissing her noisy stomach. "I am starved as well. Do you want to set snares or start the fire?" His question was asked in the same way they always worked together to complete a task.

"I'll start the fire."

He sat up, kissing her shoulder before resting his chin

there, his face so close to hers she could feel his warm breath on her neck.

"We'll have tonight, Ella."

She knew what he meant. The next day, they would return home, and things would continue to move forward.

But now, here in the woods, with only the birds and animals to witness, they would have this time together.

Later, life would intrude, but even then, as time moved on, no one could ever take this moment from them.

*

While Kieran's snares proved inefficient, he had managed to catch a few fish to roast over the fire for their meal.

They spent the evening snuggled up together on their furs, watching the stars grow brighter as the night fell around them.

"Do you remember when we were little and we would lie in the field at the top of the hill and watch the stars?" he asked her.

"It almost seemed like you could see them moving."

"Aye. I thought of it a year or so ago when I was sent to the border with a few of the men to guard against raiding. The men were talking about whatever they talk about as we settled to sleep. But as I lay there, I looked up at the stars and remembered when we were little. How we talked about everything and anything and I was never afraid to share something with you. How easy it was to be with you. How easy life was back then."

He didn't know why he mentioned it. Except that the comfort he'd always felt about sharing something with her remained all these years, and it was easy to tell her his thoughts.

"Mayhap later, when we might have reason to miss one another, we could go out at night and look up at the stars and remember this night. And how very perfect everything was for a little while at least."

He turned his head to look at her and saw a tear travel from the outer corner of her eye across her temple to be lost in her hair.

He reached over and laced his fingers with hers, giving her hand a squeeze.

"That is for tomorrow, remember? Don't let those thoughts cut our night short."

She nodded and forced a smile as she wiped at her eyes, brightened by her tears. He rolled over to kiss her. He wanted her again. He worried he would never stop wanting her like this.

Just the touch of her lips made him hard and ready.

But unlike the desperation they'd felt earlier, this was slower. They drew out every touch, every word, as if doing so would slow the moon and keep the sun from rising.

When he finally slid into her, they looked into each other's eyes and shared a smile. They didn't need words for knowing each other so well. But they didn't look away. He watched as he made love to her. Seeing every smile, hearing every gasp and moan. And he watched when her pleasure claimed her.

"Beautiful," he said.

When he climaxed, he pulled her tight to him until he knew she had fallen asleep. But he did not join her right away.

Instead, he looked up at the stars in the sky and begged them to stay where they were so he could hold Ella forever.

Chapter Seventeen

Kieran was almost surprised to see the sun when he opened his eyes the next morning. Not because he'd actually thought the stars would obey, but because they had slept well into the morning.

In fact, Ella was still asleep.

Or she was until he turned to see her more clearly.

Her eyes opened, and she looked confused for a moment before she saw him and smiled.

"I thought mayhap I had dreamed what happened between us. I had dreamed it many nights of late," she said.

He smiled. "I have dreamed of you as well. But I had

many things wrong. The real thing was so much better than my dreams."

She nodded. Then tilted her head to the side.

"Why did you never lie with another woman?"

He shouldn't have been surprised Ella would ask such an impertinent question. If she could be so brave to ask, he would be just as brave to answer.

"Because of you."

"Me?"

"Aye. Anytime I thought of it, I knew I didn't care for the women the way a man should who would do such a thing, and I thought of a man touching you and not respecting you the way he should, and I couldn't do it. I couldn't use a maid for my needs, no matter how willing she was, because I knew it would never be more."

She nodded and then frowned.

"What is it?" he asked, hoping she had no reason for regret this morning. He had none. In fact, he was trying to remember the reason why they'd agreed to only last night, for he was very much wanting to love her again before they left the peace of the forest to face the day.

"You were jealous."

He blinked, for her thoughts were not the same as his.

"You were jealous of Arran."

He let out a breath and went with the truth.

"Aye. I imagine I was. And still am in that he is free to do what he wishes, while I must do as my father bids. I envy his freedom."

"Yesterday and last night . . ." She pulled the plaid up to cover all his favorite parts of her and sat up. "I hope it wasn't just that you wished to claim something so you could have it first."

He felt his eyes go wide in surprise and reached out to place a hand on her arm.

"You know me better than anyone. Do you think that is why we . . . ?"

She gave it more time than he thought was necessary but was pleased when she eventually turned to him with a smile and shook her head.

"Nay. I don't really think that."

"Good." He leaned closer and rested his head against hers as the silence between them spun out and grew tense. "We must go."

She nodded, which caused his head to move with hers.

"Aye. We must face what comes next."

He pulled back and looked into her eyes, wanting to tell her he didn't know how. That he was frightened. He said nothing, but after a moment she reached out and put her hand on his cheek.

"Everything will be all right, Kieran."

He wanted to argue, but instead he grasped on to her words, hoping somehow they would be true.

*

Ella didn't know what to expect as they rode toward home, but she was almost surprised to learn nothing had changed between them. They still laughed and talked as they rode along. He still teased her, and she needled him with nosy questions he attempted to dodge.

It was only when they arrived and stared out over the valley where they got their first sight of Girnigoe Castle that she shivered and felt uneasy.

This was the end.

"It seems strange that I should feel the need to say goodbye," he said quietly. His voice barely heard in the breeze. "But I feel the need the same, whether I should or should not. We will still see each other in the hall and other times, but we must go back to how things were before."

"Aye. It does feel like goodbye," she agreed.

He moved his horse closer so their legs touched.

"If it is to be goodbye on what we had yesterday, might I trouble you for one last kiss?"

She leaned toward him as he did the same, and their lips touched just briefly. When they pulled apart, he gave her a stiff smile and a resigned nod.

"Thank ye, Ella."

"Thank ye, Kieran."

Without another word, they rode to the castle and through the gates. It wasn't until he reached up and helped her down from her horse that she noticed the biggest difference between them. The way his hands lingered on her body and his pale green eyes seemed to grow darker with desire.

The way her body quivered for wanting to reach out and pull him to her lips.

But, of course, she couldn't do that, and not just because they were standing in the bailey and the groom was waiting for her to hand over the reins to her horse.

They'd just said goodbye to what had been between them. It seemed a simple thing, but it was a formal closure on their passion. It had to be.

"I should get inside and see what may need to be done in the kitchens," she said, pointing at the door that led to the kitchens, as if Kieran didn't know where they were. How silly.

He nodded.

"Aye. I should see my father. I'm sure he will have questions about my travels. Or maybe he didn't even notice I was away." He smiled.

"Very well. I shall see you at the late meal, then."

"Yes. The late meal."

She hurried off and practically ran to the kitchen to get away from the urge to rush to him and wrap her arms around him.

The women eyed her suspiciously as she helped with the meal.

"It seems something has you in a lather," Marnie stated.

Ella shook her head. "Nay, I'm fine. It is only that I met someone when I was visiting my aunt, and my thoughts seem to go toward him when I least expect it."

In truth, she hadn't thought of Arran most of the day, but she knew this news would keep them from pestering her or prying in places Ella couldn't keep hidden.

She told them about Arran and allowed them to titter and speculate about what everything meant.

It was Joan who asked quietly while the others were talking among themselves about what a fine bride Ella would make, "Are ye pleased for the match? No matter how fine he may be, he is not Kieran."

Just hearing his name made her chest hurt. She refrained from placing her hand there to rub at the spot, but only barely.

She couldn't manage to answer the woman, and her silence must have served as answer enough, for Joan came closer and put an arm over her shoulders.

"It will get better, I promise ye. Soon ye will find ways to be happy again, and every day it will be easier than the last."

Ella nodded, hoping that was true.

When it was time for the meal to be served, Ella carried a tray out.

As soon as she cleared the large arched doorway, her gaze went immediately to the high table. Her heart quickened when she saw Kieran sitting there next to his father.

His gaze fell on her, and he smiled. Not his usual smile, but one that held more heat and interest. She looked away quickly so no one else would notice. She thought it strange that no one seemed to see the desire burning across the room between them.

When she returned to the kitchen, she decided to stay there rather than risk going back out into the hall where she could see Kieran.

She had never been one for hiding from a problem, but she wasn't ready to face him yet.

After cleaning up from the late meal, Ella headed for the cottage she shared with her father rather than stay for the night's entertainments. She didn't know how she would manage to sit next to Kieran and not want to touch him. The few times she'd caught him looking at her had made her stomach flutter.

She changed for bed and was about to put out the candles when her father came in, looking like a storm cloud.

"What is it? What's happened?" She lived in constant fear that her father would be pulled away to battle. Each time he was, she knew she was at risk of losing him. Warriors fell, no matter how great they were.

"I'll ask you what has happened, daughter, and I expect you to tell me the truth."

She squinted in confusion.

"What happened between ye and Kieran on your travels to visit Jenny?"

Ella gasped and put her hands to her cheeks in an effort to hide her blush. Why would he ask her such a thing unless he suspected—or unless he *knew* the truth?

"Did Kieran say something?" she asked. They'd not been home a full day and already Kieran had spilled their secret?

Her father let out a snarl.

"Nay. The man hasna been able to look me in the eye since you've returned. All afternoon when I tried to speak to him of the trip, he looked away and told me all was well. And then tonight, when you left the hall, I watched him watching you."

"He's always watched over me. He's protective. You've always said you were grateful for his constant guard."

"He wasna watching you in a protective way, lass. It was . . ." It was her father's turn to blush and look away in embarrassment. "It was the way a man looks at a woman he knows in a carnal way."

She sighed heavily. There was no reason to try to hide it now, when her father had already seen the truth. She wouldn't lie to her father if it could be helped.

"Very well. Since you know so much of it already, I will tell you. Kieran and I were together on the way back to Girnigoe."

"I'll know if he forced ye."

Ella narrowed her eyes on her father.

"You know Kieran nearly as well as I. You know he would never do such a thing."

He let out a breath. "That I do. But I never thought him to ruin ye when he's betrothed to another. He canna marry you and do right by ye. Why would he hurt ye in this way?"

"It wasn't something he took from me, da. It was something he *gave* me. Gave *us*. This one chance to be together in that way before he must marry. It is something I will treasure the rest of my days."

"And if you find another man who can give ye his heart? What will you tell him?"

"If he's willing to give me his heart, I would hope he would say he loves me regardless of whether I'm chaste or no.

Wouldn't he?"

She knew she had won that argument when he threw his hands in the air in frustration.

"I don't want this for you, Ella. To long for someone you canna have. To live with that empty pain."

"Like the empty pain you hold because of my mother?"

"When she died, she took my heart with her."

"That is not true. I know you still had a bit of it left because you gave it to me."

His anger faded, and reluctantly he reached for her and pulled her into a hug that nearly squeezed the breath from her. Teague Ross gave the very best hugs.

"I'm sorry, papa. I didn't mean to disappoint you."

"Ye haven't called me papa since you were a bairn. Don't use the word now to soften me," he growled, but when he squeezed her tighter, she knew the word had hit its mark.

She laughed against his chest.

"Very well." She stepped back to look him in the eye so he would know she meant it. "I'm sorry."

"Do you regret it?"

"Nay. Not at all."

"Then it makes no sense to apologize for it."

"I guess not." She tilted her head, looking for chinks in his armor so she might say the thing to make it right between them again. "It was the most wonderful moment of my life."

That had not been the right thing. Her father winced and shook his head.

"I don't want to hear that."

"Would you rather it had been horrible?"

"I'd rather pretend it didn't happen at all." He paced a bit in the room and then came back to stand in front of her. "Let us never speak of it again."

She pressed her lips together so as not to laugh at the desperate look in his eyes. She'd been given a weapon. With just a few words, she could bring him to his knees. But she wouldn't use it. At least not right now.

"Very well, papa. We'll not speak of it again."

He rolled his eyes and, grabbing up the pail, left to get them water for the next morning.

Her father had gone easy on her. She guessed it wouldn't be as well for Kieran.

Chapter Eighteen

After a night of tossing and turning, and wishing Ella was in his arms, Kieran gave up and went to the hall to break his fast. He hoped to see Ella and maybe share a moment of privacy with her.

He wished to kiss her again, though he knew he couldn't. It was too great a risk. Someone could see them, and she would be ruined.

But he wanted to talk with her.

They said things would go back to normal, and they had spent time together alone nearly every day, either hunting or tossing rocks into the sea.

Ella wasn't in the hall with the men. But her father was.

Kieran had not expected to have so much trouble facing the man after what had happened between Kieran and the man's daughter, but it was nearly impossible to have the war chief speak to him when Kieran held so much guilt.

He still didn't regret what he'd done with Ella, but talking with Teague as if he hadn't defiled his little girl had proved impossible.

"I'll take Kieran with me to check the southern borders, my laird," Teague said as everyone broke to go about their duties after the morning meal.

"Very well." His father waved his hand at the same time Kieran murmured a curse under his breath. A ride to check the southern border would take all day. He didn't know how he'd manage so much time alone with the man in Kieran's current state.

It was worse than the time they'd set the stable ablaze and had been forced to tell him what they'd done. Only much, much worse.

For once in his life, Kieran wished his father wanted to keep him at the castle rather than allow him to ride out with Teague. But, of course, his father wouldn't do as Kieran wanted.

In the bailey, they gathered their things for their ride.

Kieran cringed as he watched the war chief strap his large sword across his back and check the six daggers across his belt.

Kieran strapped his own sword and realized he only had two daggers with him. Should he get more? Would he need them if Teague attacked?

He didn't think himself capable of hurting the man he'd thought of as a real father. And maybe Kieran was nervous for no reason.

Ella wouldn't have told her father what they'd done. Teague might suspect something, but he didn't *know*. Kieran had never lied to the man, but in this instance at least, Kieran thought it might be warranted.

They rode out in silence, and that silence followed them on their journey. It wasn't until they stopped to water the horses and take a bit of food that Kieran gathered his courage to speak.

"You're angry at me," he said more than asked, for it was quite obvious.

The man looked out over the vast land before them for a few minutes longer before turning and squaring his gaze on Kieran's.

"I'm disappointed in you."

Kieran felt the words like a blow to his gut.

"Christ. That is even worse." Surely, the man knew

Kieran's weakness and used it against him now.

"When the two of you got back, I sensed something. The way you haven't been able to look me in the eye, the way she sent sultry looks at you last night during the meal. It didn't take much to figure it out; you're both shite at hiding it."

"It's not what you might think." Kieran raised his hand.

"I swear if you start spouting words like *most wonderful moment*, I will drop you where ye stand."

"Ella said that? That it was the most wonderful—"

At Teague's growl, Kieran cleared his throat and changed course.

"You know it was wrong. 'Tis why you can't look at me."

Kieran didn't think it had been wrong. Knowing that he and Ella both felt it was right gave Kieran the courage to stare the man down.

"I'll say I surely didn't think of you at all at the time, Teague, and while I'm not sure how to deal with you, I will never say it was wrong."

"You are to marry another."

"I know. We both knew."

"And if there is a child?"

"I took precautions." Precautions that very man had taught him when he'd come of age to show interest in the lasses.

"You played her a whore."

Kieran had drawn his dirk without thought.

"I showed her respect for a future I couldn't be a part of. And I'll not let you speak that way of it. It was not like that. It wasn't lust. It was . . ."

"It was what? *Love?*" Teague pushed as if not noticing the dirk in Kieran's hand. He probably knew well enough Kieran would never draw the man's blood. Kieran couldn't be sure if the same could be said for his own at Teague's hand.

He was like a father to Kieran, but he wasn't Kieran's father. He was Ella's, and Kieran had wronged her.

"She has been my friend for as long as I remember. She is part of my very soul. Ye can't say there is not a bond between us." Kieran squeezed the fist not holding the dagger. The scar on his palm felt hot.

"Do you plan to keep her as a leman after you're wed?"

"I'll not even answer such a question. You may not be pleased with what we did, but you know me, Teague. You know I would never disgrace Ella or my wife in such a way."

"I should go to your father and demand he make you marry my daughter for what you've done."

"And if I thought the laird would agree, I'd beg you to do just that. But we both know what lies down that path.

Everyone would know, and while it was the two of us that made the decision together, it would be Ella alone that is judged for it. So instead, I will beg you to keep this secret, to spare her the burden she shouldn't have to bear."

Teague looked miserable, and Kieran wished he could say the right thing to free them both from this turmoil.

He slipped his dirk into the sheath at his hip and held his arms out wide.

"If it would make you feel better to take a swipe at me, I—"

He didn't even get the offer out before the man swung his large fist right into Kieran's stomach, stealing his breath. The second strike landed on Kieran's jaw. He swayed for a moment before dropping to the ground.

*

Ella was leaving the kitchens when she spotted her father and Kieran leaving the stables that evening after returning from their travels to the border.

Even in the dim light, she could see Kieran's jaw was black and blue and he was holding his side, but the men were laughing, as they were accustomed to doing.

She would never understand how men so easily got over a brawl.

When Kieran saw her, he stopped and his lips pulled up in a smile. Her father, however, must have noticed his reaction, for he reached out and cuffed Kieran good in the back of the head.

"Oof. That's the last time I let you hit me without retaliation. The next time, I'll lay ye flat, old man," Kieran said with little heat.

Her father let out a huff and walked away from them.

"You could have warned me you told him," Kieran complained with an easy smile as he rubbed his jaw.

"It was you who gave us away, so you deserved whatever you got."

"I think he may have broken a rib."

"Do you want me to look at it?"

"Nay," he said too quickly.

She cocked her head at him.

"Are you worried I'll not be able to keep my wits if I were to touch you when you were not wearing a shirt?"

"It's not *your* wits that are in question."

She smiled at the compliment he'd unknowingly paid her. She rather liked the thought of him not being in control of himself when he was near her.

"I must go wash for the meal. That is, if you have saved anything back for me." He tilted his head in question.

"Of course, I have."

"Then I'll be back after a cold dip in the loch."

"Mmm." The sound slipped out as she imagined him naked with loch water trailing down his golden skin.

"I beg of ye, Ella. Never make that sound again when ye are near me."

She laughed, but when he stepped closer to her, the smile fell from her lips. He was so close she could feel his breath in her hair. She could feel his arousal pressed against her hip as she looked up at him, caught in his gaze. The light green had gone darker, for the blacks of his eyes had grown large.

She swallowed and felt the response of her body. Her breasts ached as her nipples tightened. Her heart pounded, and her breathing turned to short pants.

And just when she considered reaching up on tiptoe to kiss him, he stepped back again, leaving her chilled from the lack of his heat.

"I'll remind ye, Ellisay Carra Ross, I am not the only one of us vulnerable to such things." The smirk on his smug face reminded her of their many pranks over the years.

"And I'll remind you that I do not shy away from your threats, Kieran James Sinclair."

He growled, but it was not of anger. It was pure desire.

In the end, they managed to keep their hands off of each other for three days. It was a valiant effort but a doomed campaign, for neither of them wanted to give up the remaining time they had together.

They had agreed to go hunting one morning, fearing people would think it strange if they did not.

She did her best to keep distance between them, but while they hunted it was often easier if they were closer so they might whisper to one another without scaring their game.

She turned to tell him something at the same time he turned toward her.

They both breathed long and slow, but at the same time they lurched for each other, and soon they were on the ground rolling about and kissing.

"Damn these breeches," Kieran complained as he unfastened her falls and tugged the tight buckskins down her legs before removing her boots.

She rather enjoyed his eagerness and managed to remove her clothes in time for him to fall on her. The groan that came from them when they finally joined scared the birds from their roosts.

"Ella, I've thought of this every minute since we returned home," he said with heavy breaths.

"I haven't been able to sleep. I think of you and have to touch myself the way you touched me to relieve myself of the tension."

"Ye touch yourself?" he asked, his bright eyes even

wider with shock. When he pulled away, she nearly cried for wanting him where he was. "Show me," he demanded.

"What?" She didn't understand and was overcome by dissatisfaction when he left her body so abruptly.

"Touch yourself the way you did at night in your bed. I want to see it."

She didn't understand what was so exciting about it, but she didn't need to know why to know he found great satisfaction in watching her stroke her fingers through her folds in the way he had done.

"Christ, Ella. That is . . . I've never . . ." He squeezed his eyes shut and shook his head. "Ye must stop now, or I will be done for."

She might have pointed out it hadn't been her idea in the first place, but he grasped on to her hips and thrust inside her again, stealing away her ability to say anything but his name over and over.

After giving in during their hunt, they came up with ways to be alone nearly every day. And each day when she thought it might be enough to walk away, it only made her look forward to the next day and the next.

And soon a month was gone.

The days moved by too quickly. They were running out of time.

Chapter Nineteen

"We could run away," Kieran said one afternoon as they lay naked in the hayloft of the stables.

"What?" Ella looked at him with her brows pulled together. "Run away?"

"I don't want to marry the MacKenzie lass. I want to be with you. We could leave Girnagoe, leave Caithness, leave the Sinclair lands entirely. We could join another clan. I could be a soldier, and we could be happy."

Just thinking about it made his heart pound with longing. He wanted that simple life. Just him and Ella and whatever family they would be blessed to have in a place where he wasn't the heir.

Where he could just be Kieran.

But Ella was shaking her head. He'd thought she would be ready to pack the instant he suggested his plan, but she only put her hand on his and said, "Nay, Kieran. We can't run away."

"Why not? It would probably be weeks before my father even noticed I had left. He won't care."

"He will. You know he will. You are his heir, and he will search all the Highlands for you. And whomever is daft enough to give you refuge will be claimed as an enemy. This is your clan. You are a Sinclair, Kieran. I'll not allow you to give up your birthright because of me. It isn't right."

"What isn't right is that I'm not allowed to marry the person I want to spend my life with." He rested his palm along her cheek and tried to meet her gaze so she would agree.

She squeezed her eyes closed and shook her head as if trying to hold off his words.

"You mustn't say such a thing, Kieran. It will only make it worse."

"Not if we leave this place so we can stay together. Say you will go with me."

"I cannot. We will not find peace. We would be hunted."

Of course, he knew she was right.

He relented and held his arms out so she would come closer and he could hold her.

"Tell me you will think about it," he asked.

"Very well. I'll think about it."

"If there is a way to make this plan work, you will find it," he said and kissed her hair.

"I am the best at making plans."

He laughed sadly. When she tilted her head up to look at him, he stared into her eyes.

"I would choose you, Ella. If I could."

She smiled, though it looked painful.

"I would choose you too."

They let go of the unhappiness and plans that could never come to be in exchange for kisses and promises they wouldn't be able to keep.

An hour later, Kieran ran his hands over his hair to make sure there weren't any stray pieces of hay from his time in the loft with Ella. He pressed his lips together to keep the smile restrained before stepping into the great hall.

It wouldn't do for his father to see him happy. He would surely do his best to put an end to such a thing. No matter how it had come to be.

Kieran and Ella only had a month left before they would have to part for good. No more sneaking off together to fall into their desires. He thought again about his plan for them to leave their home and go away together and knew Ella had been right. It wouldn't work.

His father might not have wanted him to be his heir, but since he was, he would never allow him to walk away.

If Kieran was worried his father might notice his happiness, he quickly realized he had nothing to fear, for the laird was in a fit of rage. The high table had been cleared of all tankards and trenchers, which lay scattered on the floor, and one of the lower tables had been overturned.

For the slightest moment, Kieran worried that his father had learned of what was going on between he and Ella, but he knew that information would not earn this type of response.

To the laird, Ella was insignificant. His war chief's daughter. If he learned Kieran had touched her, he would easily shrug it off, as other warriors tupped the lusty maids that made eyes at them. He wouldn't see it as anything of import. Kieran would be ordered to give up such foolishness when he married.

Kieran would be expected to obey because he always obeyed.

In this, Kieran wished he could defy his father, but now obviously wasn't the time. The laird wasn't irritated at Kieran.

This was something else.

Kieran spotted the cowering messenger edging toward the door and noticed his MacKenzie plaid. A parchment was clenched in his father's fists.

Pulling the messenger aside, Kieran asked the man what it had said.

The lad clearly looked worried that Kieran might suddenly go into a rage as well. "I'm sorry. I am only doing what I was sent to do."

"What news do ye bring?"

"The laird's daughter . . . she . . . that is . . ." the young man stammered, and Kieran wanted to shake the words from him so he would know what had happened.

"What of my betrothed?" he asked again. Had she died? He didn't wish for harm to become her, but he didn't know her, and if he could be spared this marriage . . .

He shook his head, ashamed of himself.

"She's run away. Eloped. With a Campbell."

Oh. This was even better. Not only was he to be released from the marriage, but he would not face the guilt of her death.

Teague stepped into the hall and looked at the mess before walking straight to Kieran.

"What's happened?"

"My betrothed has broken the marriage contract. She's eloped with a Campbell."

"Christ," Teague whispered. "Had it been anyone but a Campbell, it might have been more acceptable."

"It could have been a MacDonald."

Both the messenger and the war chief shivered in disgust.

"I thought the Campbell laird was recently married. No son of his would be of age to marry."

"Nay," the messenger said. "She married the war chief of the clan. Who is said to be a bastard."

Teague's brows rose. "The lass has guts."

"The lass is going to start a war," the messenger responded quietly while taking in the sight of the laird throwing a bench against the wall.

"We must do something," Teague said.

"What do you have in mind?"

"Go talk to him."

"You said *we* must do something."

"I'll see you properly buried afterward." Teague winked, but Kieran couldn't be so sure the man spoke in jest. After all, he had ruined the chief's daughter.

Kieran took a moment to consider his options. It wasn't that his father would like him less for Kieran tackling him to the ground, but Kieran did worry his father wouldn't need much reason to pull a blade on him to be done with him.

It would have to be reasoning, then.

"Father," Kieran called out as he strode toward the smaller man.

Right away, his father paused and turned his glare upon Kieran.

"This is all your fault."

"Of course, it is," Kieran muttered to himself. Clearing his throat, he spoke louder. "I'm sure we will be able to move on from this."

"We can't allow another clan to steal from us."

Steal? It only took Kieran a moment to recall that the MacKenzies had taken half of the settled-upon cattle with them when they'd left. And now that there would be no marriage, they would be required to return them.

"He's sold off some of the cattle, and some were taken in a raid. He says he'll be unable to return them."

His father didn't care how Kieran might have been affected by losing his bride, it all came down to the cattle and his father's integrity as a fierce and imposing laird.

"What is to be done, then? Do we go to war on the MacKenzies for thieving our cattle in a more friendly manner than others have done in the past? It's the Highlands; everyone steals cattle from their neighbors. It's a way of life."

"We won't be waging war on the MacKenzies." His father let out a deep breath and turned to the messenger. "Tell your laird we shall meet him, and he should ready his army to join us as we wage war on the Campbells."

"The Campbells? Why would we go to war with them? They don't have our cattle."

"Nay. But they have your betrothed. The man who married her will either have the marriage annulled, so you can go forward with the wedding, or risk war with two clans. He'll see the error and make it right."

His father calmed down and pointed at the mess on the floor.

"Have this mess cleaned up," he snapped and rushed off toward his study.

Kieran turned to Teague, who shook his head and walked away.

Kieran gave a broken piece of wood a swift kick and slumped onto a bench.

He couldn't believe how horrid his luck was. He'd wanted a way to get out of this marriage, and it had been delivered to him. Yet his father would not let it go.

Kieran was doomed to seek vengeance for a grievance he welcomed with his whole heart. He wondered what he had done to be punished so. Was he to face judgment for his mother's crimes and live a life of constant unhappiness? Even worse because he knew well what happiness felt like only to have it snatched away.

"Bloody hell." He tossed another chunk of wood and

went to ready himself for battle to get back the woman he didn't want.

*

Ella was alerted that something was amiss when the maids came in whispering and gathering food.

Salted meat and bannocks were saved for soldiers if they were traveling for war.

She left the kitchen to find the hall broken. Had someone attacked them?

But there were no men in the hall fighting.

She raced out to the bailey to find them there. Her father was calling out orders to his men to gather their weapons. The grooms were bringing out horses already covered in armor.

There had not been a battle in the hall, but there was to be a battle.

"What has happened?" she asked one of the men who was filling a knapsack with food.

"Isla MacKenzie has married a rotting Campbell."

It took a moment for Ella to realize why that name was familiar.

"Kieran's intended?"

"Aye. The laird sees the disregard of the marriage

contracts as an act of war by the Campbells. We plan to use a show of force to get the Campbells to concede."

"I see." Ella felt as if she'd been punched in the stomach.

All this fuss because a woman married another? Kieran would be free of the marriage he didn't want, yet she saw him across the courtyard tucking daggers into his sash.

She made her way over to him. When he saw her, his shoulders seemed to slump and he didn't raise his head to meet her eyes.

"You're going to fight to get your bride back," Ella said, hating that she sounded jealous. She'd known all along he would marry, and she'd promised herself she wouldn't pine for the man once that happened.

But it hadn't happened yet, and it seemed the woman didn't want to marry him any more than Kieran wanted to marry her.

"It is not my choice. My father has called us to arms, so we will go and fight if needed. But it shouldn't come to that. The Campbells won't risk losing men for one lass. She will be made to honor the marriage contract."

"Then you should go get her."

"Ella," he said, pain clear in his voice as he finally raised his head to look her in the eye. "Ye know this is not what I want. But my father will not let this offense go. She will be found, and I will be wed."

Ella nodded. She might have known this was how it would be, but she'd had no idea how much it would hurt.

Chapter Twenty

Kieran had put off this moment for as long as possible, but it was time to say goodbye to Ella. And in so doing, he would destroy a friendship they'd had all their lives.

But there was nothing for it. When he returned with his bride, everything between he and his best friend would need to be put aside. All hope of continuing their friendship had died when he continued to give into his desires over and over again. He may not know Isla MacKenzie, and he surely didn't love her. But he would not be an unfaithful lout of a husband.

Even if it didn't bear well that his bride had run off to

marry another.

He was bound by honor to a woman who was a stranger to him, despite his love for the woman he knew better than any other person.

He would not carry on with Ella when he could not offer himself fully. She deserved more than a shameful affair. She deserved a happy life. If she found that happiness with Arran Sutherland, Kieran would be pleased for them. Eventually.

Ella stood before him, a strand of her hair falling over her temple, curling against her face. He wanted to reach out and brush it back, but he dared not for what that simple act would do to him.

"You are ready?" she asked, and he saw a small tremor at her bottom lip. He wasn't sure if she was asking if he was ready for the battle or ready to move on with his life. The truth was he'd rather face a thousand battles if it meant getting to keep this woman.

He simply nodded.

He knew she was putting on a brave face when really she wished to cry. He silently thanked her for her bravery. For if she broke down, he would give in and pull her into his arms, and all would be lost. For a while at least.

But his father would eventually win. There was no doubt in that. Kieran would marry this MacKenzie lass in the end. He squeezed his fingers into fists at his side.

"I am." He nodded again and pressed his lips together to hold in the words he wanted to speak. That he loved her. That he didn't want to go. If he begged her to run away again, would she be desperate enough to consider it? And if she did, what kind of life would that be?

"I wish you well. If my da doesn't think this will end in bloodshed, then it should be a simple thing. When the force of two armies shows up to collect your bride, the Campbells will surely have no choice but to turn her over with apologies."

Again, Kieran nodded. "It is what my father has said as well." Of course, Kieran had mixed feelings about the lack of a battle. He thought he might like a fight to purge him of all his anger.

"Do you regret it?" she asked, not needing to explain what she meant.

"Never. No matter how much it hurts at the moment." He shook his head. "We knew this was going to happen all along. I thought we would have more time, but with this battle, plans have changed."

She nodded again, but the motion was jerky, as if she were made of wood.

"I'm sorry, Ella. I wish . . ." He shook his head. "It doesna matter what I wish, does it? I hope you find happiness, Ella. And know that I will always remember that night when I look at the stars. I will always think of you."

The horns sounded, and the gates opened to let the soldiers out of the bailey.

"I must go," he said, making no move to leave. He raised his hand as if to touch her but let it drop to his side.

"I hope she is not a hag," Ella said, making him smile at the memory of his worries. As their laughter faded, they exchanged a look that communicated all the things they couldn't say.

She loved him.

He loved her.

Rather than acknowledge such a thing when there was nothing to be done for it, he cleared his throat and said, "I will see you when I return."

She nodded, but the way she looked away, he wondered if he would. He didn't push for the truth.

"Aye. I'll see you when you return," she answered.

With those lies spoken, she reached up on her tiptoes and placed a kiss on his cheek. He wanted for all the world to seize her in his arms and deepen the kiss until they could both be lost in their love, but he allowed her to step back and then turn away from him so he could leave.

Anger, the likes of which he had never felt in his life, washed through him, making his blood run like fire in his veins as he wrenched the reins to Ridire from the groom and tossed himself up into his saddle. With one final look at her, he reared the beast toward the gate that was opening.

Teague called something to him, but he didn't hear as he raced from the castle, across the drawbridge and into the field. Giving Ridire his head, they flew over Sinclair lands alone, the wind rushing in his ears turning to whispers that he needed to stop and wait for the rest of their army. That his father would not be pleased he had left like this.

It was then, thinking of how he would once again earn his father's ire, that he found the source of his rage. He hated his father.

All his life Kieran had continued his attempts to earn favor with the man who could barely look at him. He had avoided his father and even disliked him, but now, all the pain the man had inflicted burned with the heat of a thousand suns and forged into hatred.

If Kieran stopped to wait for the man to catch up to him, he just might find a sword in his hand and his father's blood pooling at his feet.

Nay, this was better. He would ride through his anger so he wouldn't do something unforgivable.

*

Ella should have said something. She should have

wished him happy. Should have told him she understood. Should have told him she changed her mind and wished to run away with him. She should have simply said goodbye. But she stood there in numb silence as tears rolled down her cheeks and dripped from her chin onto her kirtle.

The look on his face as he had ridden out of the bailey had scared her. She'd never seen him in so much pain. And she would not be the one to ease his pain ever again.

Her father rode over to her and frowned when he saw her tears.

"Come now, Ella. Ye knew this was how it would go."

"I know." She wiped the tears away.

"But still, it pains ye."

"Aye." She wiped the new tears away and offered a shaky but brave smile. "I will be fine so long as you promise to come home."

"Ye know I don't make such promises, lass, except to say I'll do my best. But I have always come home so far. This will be no different. It will not come to a fight. It will all be settled in words. But we have the MacKenzie warriors with us if it comes to swords, and we will easily win against the Campbells. The Campbell laird will never side with his chief if it means war. It will be over quickly. We are certain of it."

"And if you win, it means . . . I lose."

"Yes, Kieran will be married to the MacKenzie lass as

soon as the annulment is complete. Rolfe won't risk a delay."

"I want to be the stalwart friend when he returns with his bride, but I do not think I can stand to see him again. I fear having to sit at the feast will thoroughly break my already severely chipped heart."

Teague nodded. "Then you should go back to Jenny. She wrote and told me a certain Sutherland lad has been asking after ye. Jenny told me if he were to ask for your hand I was to say yes. Even still, I wrote to William to get his opinion of the lad, and he speaks highly of the man. Perhaps your future happiness lies in Kildary."

"I can't imagine having to spend my life with a war chief," she said, making it seem like the worst possible future. Her father laughed at her, as she had hoped.

"Can he make you happy?" he asked, serious once more.

"I think, maybe, one day Arran Sutherland could make me happy. If I could allow myself to let go of the person I can't have."

"I've spent the last twenty years watching a good friend cleave to what he lost and turn away from everything that might bring him happiness." Her father glanced over to where the laird was being armored. "I don't want that for you, Ella. Kieran was never to be yours."

"I know. I have known that all my life. And I thought I

had done a good job of keeping him in a place where I would not want more. But it just happened without my allowing it."

Her father pulled her close and kissed the top of her head.

"Aye. These things have a habit of sneaking up on us when we are not looking and catching us unaware. But you can move on and find the person who is meant to be yours. If this Arran offers for you, and Jenny likes him, then I approve of the match. Ye can tell my sister I said so—not that she would care what I say."

Ella nodded.

"Perhaps if we wed as soon as I arrive, I will be able to avoid this pain. Being married must be better than being left behind when Kieran marries."

"Give yourself some time to heal before you move on. Or at least enough time to know you are doing it for the right reason. There is no set time for these things. And it isn't fair to this Arran to be used to save you from heartache."

"You never moved on from mama," she pointed out.

He shrugged. "That was not because I couldn't. I had you, and mayhap I was too stubborn to have to change our ways to accommodate another person in our lives."

"A stubborn Scot? I've never heard of such a thing."

They shared a shaky laugh, and she turned serious again.

"Do you think you might be ready to look for someone to spend the rest of your life with after I go off to Kildary?"

"Perhaps. I'll miss you something awful. I may come visit you and never leave. But first I must see to the Campbells."

She nodded.

"I will wish ye well. And I will see you when you come to Kildary to visit."

"Aye. I'll leave Horrace behind to escort ye to the Ross keep."

"Thank you for understanding. Please don't tell Kieran I don't plan to return. It is best this way."

"From the looks of things, I may not see him until we get to the Campbells." He frowned at the gate where Kieran had gone. "I'm sorry you're hurting, love. I hope you will find happiness at Kildary."

She wished for the same but worried it would be impossible to find happiness in Kildary when her heart remained here with Kieran Sinclair.

When all the soldiers had gone, Ella didn't return to the kitchens. She couldn't for fear she might break down into a mess of tears if someone so much as looked at her. Instead, she left through the postern gate and headed for the beach.

There, in the place where she and Kieran had shared their every secret, she screamed out at the angry sea, hoping the crashing waves would take her pain with them when they returned to the ocean.

She slumped down among the sand-smoothed rocks, sobbing and screaming until she was thoroughly spent.

When she was able to stand and see where she was going, she headed toward the cottage she'd shared with her father. She packed up her few belongings and left her home.

Forever.

Chapter Twenty-One

Kieran's anger eventually faded as he made his way to the place where the Sinclair army was making camp. Finding Teague amongst the men, Kieran let out a sigh, prepared to hear the man's words before he spoke them.

"The laird wishes to see ye."

"Of course, he does." Kieran checked his temper to make certain it was safe before he trudged off to find his father. The laird was standing on a rise, overseeing the work below, his white-blond hair flowing out behind him like a Norse god.

Having heard Kieran approach, he turned to set his icy

blue glare on him.

"Was that outburst necessary?" he asked.

"Wasn't a matter of whether it was necessary or not," Kieran answered, his earlier anger with the man flaring back to life.

This conversation would not be a passive one. Though Kieran didn't think he was in danger of injuring the leader of his clan, he was in no mood to bow down to the man who had ruined his life.

"You will marry the MacKenzie lass," he said and waited, as if expecting Kieran to argue, though he never had in the past. Perhaps the laird felt the change in Kieran as well.

When Kieran didn't answer, Rolfe continued. "Unless she is already with child. We'll not raise a Campbell mutt as one of us. But once we have ensured she is not carrying, you will wed."

Kieran kept his gaze on the field below, not seeing any of the activity. When the silence continued, Kieran decided it would fall to him to break it.

"I know my duty. I am prepared to do it." Even if it was at the greatest cost. His soul. "Though I would point out the lass must be in love to have taken so great a risk."

Kieran found himself rather impressed that she seemed stronger than he was to fight for something she wanted.

"It is of no matter."

Kieran sniffed and shook his head. What were the feelings of his potential bride when the Sinclair laird wanted something? But it wasn't just her that had taken this great risk.

"The Campbell clan has refused to give her up, choosing her happiness regardless of war."

"It won't come to war. We need only make a show of force so they will see we will not bend. No one takes from the Sinclairs. You'll never be a good laird if ye don't understand that."

Kieran couldn't help the bark of laughter that escaped his throat.

"I would think a *good* laird would see the men at his back and decide rightly if this fight was worth their lives. I would think a *good* laird would ask his son what he wanted, to at least feign a thought for his happiness despite the duty that's been heaped upon his shoulders from the moment of his first breath. Ye, father, are *not* a good laird. You are a bitter shell of a man who feels only pain, and as such chooses to inflict pain on others so he might not feel so utterly alone. Ye are not a good laird. Ye are pathetic."

He had never seen his father so shaken with surprise. The shock lasted but a moment before the familiar glare settled in once more.

"I'll not have the likes of you talk to me in that way."

"The likes of me?" It was Kieran's turn to be

surprised, but he shouldn't have been. "You mean born from my mother, of which I had no choice. I didn't wish to be brought into this world. I certainly don't mean to be a constant reminder of your loss and the fact that your beloved son is dead, leaving you with me. I don't mean to hurt you, so could you please stop punishing me for existing?"

By the end of his statement, he was shouting and his hand was shaking with the strength it took not to pull the sword from the sheath across his back.

Rather than risk losing control, Kieran turned and walked away without bothering to be dismissed.

He ran into Teague along the path down to the field.

The war chief stood there with his bulging arms crossed.

Kieran waited for him to lay into him about respect for the laird, but instead Teague gave a nod of what Kieran thought was approval and let him pass without comment.

Rather than continue up the craggy path toward the laird, Teague turned to walk down with him.

"I'm proud of ye for standing your ground with your father. It has been a long time coming."

Kieran let out a breath and shrugged. He was suddenly exhausted.

"It doesn't change anything. I'm still on this course when I'd much rather be with—" He cut himself off, unable to say her name.

But Teague allowed no escape. "Ella?"

"Aye. I know you don't wish to hear this, but I love her. I imagine I have always loved her, which could be why I hadn't noticed until now. It wasn't something I went from not doing to doing. It grew so slowly—just one day it was there."

"I'm sorry you are hurting, and for what it's worth, I do like hearing that you love her. Especially knowing what happened between you. I know you've never been a man to take advantage of a lass, but I had not been pleased to learn . . . Well, anyway, hearing your feelings on the matter and to know you are hurting as much as she is, it heals the part of me that wanted to run you through with a rusty dirk."

Kieran's eyes went wide until Teague broke into laughter. Then Kieran laughed with him.

When they quieted, Teague said, "You were wrong."

Ah. Here would come the lecture. The chief would want Kieran to apologize.

"I'll not apologize to him."

"Nay. What I mean is, it *did* change something. Between you and your da. He heard your words. You've forced him to think about things he'd refused to consider before."

"But we will still continue on for the Campbells come morning."

"Aye. I didn't say it changed your fate, just that he heard ye."

Kieran didn't know why that mattered. And didn't care enough to ask.

He wouldn't have Ella.

*

Ella arrived at Kildary two days later. She imagined Kieran, her father, and the rest of the warriors had met up with the MacKenzies and were even now moving toward the Campbell lands.

Jenny opened the door of her cottage with a wide smile and a hug. She was looking even better than when they'd last left her.

"You seem fully recovered from your illness. Your color is better," Ella noted.

"Aye. It was nothing, but I will feign sickness in the future if it means I get more visits from ye. Come, I've just made your favorite berry tarts."

Seeing how happy her aunt was to see her lessened the burden on her heart. Ella didn't feel so much as if she might burst into tears at any moment.

"I'm glad you are happy to see me, for I don't plan to leave again."

Jenny turned quickly, making her skirts swish.

"You're staying here with me?"

"Well, I am rather hoping the Ross war chief might ask for my hand, and if so, I would be living with him, but aye, I plan to stay at Kildary regardless."

Jenny pressed her lips together and came to pull her into another hug. This one was less celebration and more sympathy. Ella couldn't stand it.

Pulling away quickly, she affixed a proper smile on her face and nodded.

"It will be wonderful. Don't you always say the worst things are better when you face them with a smile?"

"And marrying Arran would be the worst thing?" Jenny asked with a slight wince.

"Nay, of course not. I would be lucky if he were to ask for my hand." She tried to feel lucky. Tried to pretend this was the life she wanted rather than the life that would keep her from melting away into a shell of herself.

"I don't think there is much question about his feelings. The two times I've seen him since you left, he's asked after you. I believe the boy is smitten."

Ella hoped she would be smitten. It wasn't fair to go into this marriage comparing Arran to the person she had known and loved all her life. Not when she had only spent such a short amount of time with him.

She liked Arran. And was sure she just needed time to fall in love with him.

"I believe we should take our meal in the hall this evening. Let us change and make our way up to the castle."

Ella nodded and rested her hand over her stomach, wondering if she would be able to eat a thing. Her stomach seemed to be tying itself into knots as she changed, and those knots became even more knotted as they walked toward the castle.

"You are walking even slower than me, and I'm an old woman."

Ella laughed. "You are not old, auntie. You only have the tiniest of gray in your hair, and your eyes are bright with mischief." There were some lines at her eyes from all the time she spent smiling, but that was a sign to anyone she was a witty person.

"Now that I'll be living here, I plan to find a man for ye," Ella promised her aunt.

"Nay. I don't want a man. I'm set in my ways." Jenny held up her hands.

"That's the same excuse my father gave. He didn't want a woman to come into our lives and change us. But I think such a change can be a good thing. I'll see you both happy."

"Mayhap you should see yourself happy first." Jenny

lifted a knowing brow.

Ella nodded and then stopped walking, causing her aunt to stop as well.

"If it should be that Arran does not ask for my hand, might I stay with you anyway?"

"You always have a home with me, niece."

Feeling better, Ella continued on to the castle . . . and a life she hoped she would come to love.

*

The late morning air was heating up with noon approaching. Kieran felt a trickle of sweat meander down his back under his armor. All around him it was quiet but for the scraping of metal, the subtle squeak of leather, and the panting of horses.

They had arrived.

Across the field from them, a handful of men waited. Not an army. Three men stood apart from the other two. They didn't even wear armor as they sat, in what appeared to be easy calm, upon their horses. Waiting.

"As I predicted, they wish to talk. They will bend to our wishes, and we will return home with my son's bride," Rolfe said to the men near enough to hear.

Kieran had kept his distance from his father since their

heated discussion days before. To Kieran's surprise, his father hadn't sent for him or ordered him to sit beside him for meals.

"Teague and Kieran will join me. They have five men. We will meet them with but three." As if this proved the Sinclairs to be fiercer in some way.

Kieran reined in his horse next to Teague, but as they traveled into the field, Rolfe moved ahead and toward the center of their group.

They came to a stop in front of the three men. Two of them older, while the last seemed to be the same age as Kieran.

"Welcome to our lands, Laird Sinclair."

"I did not come for a visit. I have come to get what was contracted to us."

The younger blond warrior shifted in his saddle, and Kieran saw his fist clench. This was the man who had married Kieran's intended. Kieran wasn't surprised to see the man didn't like for his wife to be referred to as a thing.

Could his father have stated their claim in a worse way?

"She is my wife," the blond man spoke.

Kieran waited for his father to rebuke the man's claim and state his order that the woman be handed over to them, but there was only silence from the place next to him.

Kieran turned to make sure his father was still there.

He was, but he appeared to be frozen as he stared at

the man who had spoken.

Kieran looked to Teague to determine what should be done. The war chief only shrugged as if to say he didn't know.

"Father?" Kieran whispered only loud enough to call his attention, but the large blond man turned to look at him. His eyes narrowed on Kieran, and his horse shifted a step closer.

Staring at him as he was, waiting for the man to make a movement of battle, Kieran got a better look at the war chief who had married his betrothed. The blond hair had been noticeable from afar, but this close, Kieran could see the color of his eyes. The lightest of blue. Like looking at the sky through a piece of ice.

The same color as the man sitting next to him, who finally spoke.

"You there, what is your name?" he shouted, though they were not so far away.

The men looked to one another in confusion before the man in the middle spoke.

"I am the Campbell laird. This is my brother Donal, and my war chief and brother Aiden."

"Aiden?" Rolfe said as he got down from his horse. As he walked toward them, he removed his helm.

The men gasped as Rolfe walked closer to Aiden.

"How old are ye, Aiden?"

Aiden looked to the Campbell laird for direction. The laird nodded.

"I am likely five and twenty."

"Likely? Why do you not know?" Rolfe snapped.

The Campbell laird took over when it seemed Aiden wasn't going to.

"Aiden was found wandering in this very field when he was maybe four summers. My father raised him with my brother and myself as one of his own."

Kieran suffered a wave of dizziness as he made the same calculations he guessed his father had made.

"Do ye have a scar here?" Rolfe demanded, pointing to his forearm just below his elbow. "And a mark, nay, two freckles on the back of your neck? One bigger on the right?"

"Father," Kieran called as the Campbell men looked at him as if he were mad. But Rolfe didn't pay him any attention.

"Show me. Show me your arm and the back of your neck."

Again, Aiden looked to his laird, who nodded.

Rolling back the cuff to his shirt, he held out his arm, which had a scar in the very place Rolfe had inquired. When Aiden saw it, he seemed surprised.

Kieran knew well how a warrior bore many scars. It wasn't feasible to keep track of them all.

He then twisted and pulled down the back of his shirt,

and from where Kieran sat on his horse, he could well see two dark marks. One bigger to the right of the other.

"Brody," Rolfe whispered. "My son. I've found ye."

Chapter Twenty-Two

When Ella and her aunt entered Balnagown Castle, Uncle William came to greet her. Right away, Arran was by her side, offering to escort her to the high table to take the seat next to his.

"It is a shame you only see to join us when we have guests, sister," William said to Jenny, who gave him a shove in the way brothers and sisters do.

"I was hoping you would come for a visit soon," Arran said quietly beside Ella, his gray-blue eyes studying her. "I asked after you with your aunt."

"She told me."

"Can I hope that is the reason you returned so soon?"

"It may be," she said while looking away in what she hoped was a flirtatious way.

"And where is your escort this evening?" he asked as his gaze darted around the hall.

"Kieran was unable to escort me this time. My father sent one of his other warriors."

She didn't think she imagined Arran's smile grew wider with this news.

They chatted as they ate, paying little attention to anyone else in the hall. Not until the laird called for a group of musicians to begin playing.

"Would you care to go for a walk on the battlements? It is a fair night," Arran suggested.

"I would like that."

He helped her to her feet and escorted her through the hall to the steep steps that would take them to the top of the castle.

He was right, the night was mild. Just the slightest chill to the air. Not like at Girnagoe, where the sea air whipped harshly at anyone silly enough to brave the battlements. But while the cool, damp breeze wasn't uncomfortable, she did find she already missed the salty smell of home.

Here at Balnagown, it seemed so quiet. Awkwardly so.

"I am very glad you have come to visit so soon,"

Arran said, pulling her attention from her wandering thoughts.

"Actually, it is not a visit. I have come to stay."

This seemed to surprise him, but if his smile was any indication, it was a pleasant surprise.

The silence returned, and she wondered what he was thinking, for it was clear he was pondering something of great import. How strange it was not to know someone well enough to discern their thoughts without them having to share them aloud.

But, of course, that was how it was with everyone besides Kieran.

"I know you have only just returned and that we did not have much time together during your last visit, but I do wonder . . ."

Surely, he wasn't planning to ask her to marry him now. So soon. Too soon. But then this was what she had wanted, so what did the timing matter? Still, it was certainly too soon. That couldn't be what he was wondering.

"If one wanted to speak to one's father regarding his daughter's hand, how would one find him?"

Ach. He *was* going to ask now.

She forced herself to remain calm and stay where she was. There would be no good end to running down the stairs only to fall and break her neck.

She looked up in order to settle her chaotic thoughts

and spotted the stars glittering down at her. Instantly, she was caught in the memory of that night with Kieran. The night they had promised to never forget.

Closing her eyes, she locked the memory away so she might answer this man's question. The man before her who was interested in being her husband. Whose heart was available.

She found she appreciated the way Arran spoke, as if he were speaking of someone else besides them. She decided to continue in the same manner to allow a much-needed distance from the conversation.

"When one's father knows he'll not be available, it is generally recommended that one's father allow one's *aunt* the duty of the giving of his daughter's hand in his stead."

"I see. That is even more fortunate if one is a particular favorite of one's aunt and was quite nervous about meeting one's father."

They broke into laughter. She was enjoying the twisted conversation despite the topic. But then his gaze turned serious as he looked into her eyes.

"Do you agree that before one speaks to anyone else about a woman's hand, he should ask her?"

"Aye, I do think that would be the way one would ensure the woman feels she has some control in her own fate."

He smiled and leaned closer. Taking her hand, he bent

over it to place a soft kiss across her knuckles.

"Would you marry me, Ella?" he asked quietly.

So much for too soon. It was done. He had asked. It was what she had hoped for the entire journey to Kildary. She would not need to be alone with a broken heart that would never mend. She could have a happy life with her husband and a family of her own.

She nodded, and then around the lump that suddenly grew in her throat she squeaked, "Aye."

He leaned down to kiss her then, though she noticed he didn't need to lean quite so far as Kieran had.

And if the kiss didn't inspire a sizzle of heat up her spine or a fluttering in her stomach, she decided not to notice.

She would be happy.

*

The field where the Sinclairs planned to wage war was silent.

For a moment, no one moved or spoke. As if all of them were solidified in ice. Finally, Aiden—or rather Brody, for he bore the marks Rolfe remembered of his son—turned to his brothers and spoke.

"Can this be?"

The Campbell laird looked between the men and then

nodded.

"I believe it is true, Aiden. The man looks just like you. And you have marks just where he said ye would. You've found your family."

Slowly, Brody got down from his horse and stepped forward, pulling Rolfe into an awkward hug. More surprising was that Kieran's father hugged him back. Not some soft pat, but a hearty embrace.

Kieran had not known his father knew how to do such a thing, for he'd never once ever offered Kieran a hug. Even as a boy, he'd never seen such emotion.

As if that weren't enough of a shock, Rolfe laughed. Laughed! While at the same time wiping tears from his eyes.

Who was this man who'd inhabited his father's body?

"Does this mean you will not try to take my wife from me?" Brody asked.

Once again, Rolfe broke out in laughter.

"Nay. For the MacKenzie lass has married my heir, as contracted. No agreement has been broken."

Kieran gasped as if he'd been kicked in the gut.

This man. This stranger, who looked like a younger version of his sire, was the rightful heir.

In the space of a few moments, Kieran had lost his bride, his birthright, and any reason for his father to need him for anything.

The Campbell laird chuckled.

"What started as war has turned into a time for celebration. Let's return to the castle for a proper feast."

"I have so many questions," Brody said, seemingly stunned.

"As do I. But let's go to the castle, where we can learn the answers over a tankard of ale."

Teague looked over to Kieran, but Rolfe didn't spare a glance in Kieran's direction. Why would he? He'd found his beloved son.

Kieran rode woodenly on the outside of their group. In the bailey, he had to focus on his movements while getting down from Ridire so he wouldn't fall on his arse.

"Your retainers can sit below." The Campbell laird gestured toward the great hall. "The lairds will sit at the high table in a place of honor," he spoke to Rolfe and the MacKenzie laird, who still seemed a bit confused about what had come to be.

Kieran stood there, wondering if his father even remembered him.

"This is Kieran, the laird's other son," Teague said.

Everyone turned to him as if just noticing him. Brody was the one to speak.

"I have another brother."

Kieran stood there as Brody grasped him in a hug. For

as strange as it felt to Kieran, Brody seemed not to notice, so at ease he was with hugging and being hugged.

"You should sit with us. I have questions for ye as well," the man said eagerly.

Brody sat to the right of Rolfe, with his wife, Isla, on his other side. Kieran took the seat next to her. It seemed symbolic that Kieran be at the end of the table with the rightful heir in place next to the laird.

"I'm sorry I didn't wish to marry ye," Isla told him with a wince. "When my da told me he was to marry me to ye, I realized how much I loved Aiden and needed to be with him. My father would have never allowed the match, so we took matters into our own hands."

Kieran nodded. "No offense, but I didn't wish to marry ye either."

She laughed and patted his arm.

"And now I am your sister."

He thought she would make a much better sister than a wife.

Kieran found he envied his brother. Not the attention he had received from the Sinclair laird or taking Kieran's birthright, but for the way he and Isla had rebelled and married because they couldn't be apart from each other. No matter the cost.

Wine was passed around, and while Kieran normally

didn't care much for being drunk, he welcomed the opportunity to be at least a little numb.

"So please tell me what happened that put me on the path to the Campbells," Brody said their father. Kieran set down his tankard and leaned closer, wanting to hear the story as well.

For all the times Kieran had asked his father for the truth about his mother to settle the many rumors, Rolfe had never deigned to speak of the matter.

But now, being asked by his beloved son, the laird began to speak.

"I loved your mother so very much. Muriel was my heart. When she told me she was increasing, I worried that I'd not be able to love a child as much as her. But somehow when you were born, my heart grew to love you as well.

"Your mother and I doted on you something awful; we were certain you would be spoiled. She always said she needed to give you a brother or sister so you wouldn't grow up to think you were the center of the world. And one day, when you were two, instead of saying she needed to give you a brother or sister, she told me you were going to have a brother or sister in the spring.

"Of course, I was near to bursting with happiness. I had everything I could ever want. I was laird with a loyal wife at my side who would fill the castle with children. I didn't even consider I could lose everything, everyone I loved so quickly.

"The babe came too early, a girl. Your mother and I were heartbroken over the loss, but then she developed a fever, and only a week later I lost her as well. I was inconsolable. If not for you, I might have walked into the waves and given myself up to the sea. But I couldn't leave you alone.

"I took to drinking to numb the pain. My men would carry me off to my bed each night. I'm not exactly sure what happened, but a woman came to my bed. It was hazy, but I recalled parts of that night. Wanting to let go of the pain for a short time. Months later, she returned and told me she was carrying my child."

Kieran felt more than saw Brody turn from their father to look at him. The child that was the result of a drunken seduction. Unwanted.

"I married Anna, as was right. She bore Kieran, and I was sure I had been tricked. For as much as you looked like me, Kieran did not. Not at all. But there was nothing to be done for it. We were married, and Kieran had been claimed as my child, whether he was or not."

Kieran sucked in a breath, hoping he wasn't about to learn he was not his father's child. As if this day had not already been a kick to the cods, he didn't think he could take much more.

"Now, I see myself in him. Not my coloring, but the set of his lips. The dimple in his chin. I know he is mine. But back then, I wasn't sure. And you were the child born from the woman I loved.

"Anna became jealous of how little time I spent with Kieran. In truth, I hadn't spent as much time with you when you'd been a babe either. But at almost four, you were chattering away. You always said something to make me smile. Something I'd thought I'd never do again.

"But I was called away to join the Sutherlands in a battle against the MacDonalds, and when I came back, you were gone. At first, Anna told me you had caught a fever and died, but no healer confirmed her story and there was no body. Eventually, she admitted that she wasn't watching and you were taken by the sea.

"I was so angry at her for not tending you, for allowing you to be harmed. I banished her to go live somewhere else. I didn't care where she went, I just couldn't stand to look at her. But rather than leave, she jumped from the battlements to her death."

Brody cleared his throat and picked up the story from his perspective.

"Two men took me away. They said I was to go with them to see you. But I didn't know them. One night, I heard them fighting over who would be tasked with killing me and who would have the duty to hang me on the enemy's lands. They said the laird would need to see the body as he returned home. I slipped away while they slept and hid. The next day when they called for me, I didn't move."

"You were always a smart lad," the laird said. Brody seemed to startle, as if he'd forgotten he was telling a story from the past.

"I saw other men come by where I hid, and then I heard fighting. None of the men came back. I waited, but I grew hungry. I was found wandering on the Campbell lands. The Campbell laird raised me with his children." He nodded toward the other laird and Donal.

"I didn't know to look for you. All this time, I thought you were gone. But now I wonder if Anna didn't plan to kill you and blame it on an enemy clan so we would go to war. If I died in battle, Kieran would have been laird, but since he was a child, it would have been Anna who would have had control over the clan. When her plans didn't work, she killed herself rather than tell me of her plot. I remember she had two brothers. I didn't know what had happened to them. I never cared. Of course, I didn't care about much of anything after you were gone."

"But you had Kieran," Brody said with the innocence of someone who had been accepted by strangers and assumed such a loving father would cleave to the child that had remained.

Perhaps it was the wine, or maybe the weight of the day, but Kieran laughed. A bitter sound filled with pain. But before Kieran risked exploding in anger, he pushed away from the table and left the hall. Brody said his name, but Kieran kept walking.

Unfamiliar with the Campbell lands, he managed to find his way to the loch. He laughed at the stony shore. So much like the beach at home. But unlike the churning waves of the sea, the lake was still and quiet.

Kieran scooped up a rock and tossed it in, wanting to disrupt the stillness, shatter that peace. He wished for the roar of the ocean instead of the quiet of the leaves rustling in the light breeze.

He wasn't alone for long. At the sound of footsteps he turned, wishing with his whole heart he would turn and see Ella's understanding smile.

Instead, it was his brother.

Chapter Twenty-Three

Kieran watched as Brody came closer and picked up a stone. Seeing the man's movements reminded him of his own. It was odd to see so much of himself in this stranger.

"This is one of my favorite places," Brody said. "I come here when I need to think. I toss rocks into the water, and it brings me peace."

Kieran nodded.

"At home, there is a similar place. A beach worn rough by the ocean. My . . ." He paused and attempted to find the correct word to describe Ella.

Friend.

Lover.

Other half of my soul.

"It's the place where the woman I have loved all my life and I talk about . . . well . . . everything. Small things that don't seem worth the effort of talking about and things so big there are no words."

"It sounds wonderful. I haven't known my Isla but a year, though I understand of what you speak. I often feel like she is the only person who really knows me. Many times, she's been able to soothe my worries before I've even told her the extent of them."

Kieran nodded. How many times had Ella picked up with a conversation in the middle of his thoughts?

Brody frowned.

"I'm sorry that I seem to be taking everything that was meant for you."

"You're the firstborn. The rightful heir. I've never seen father so happy." Kieran shook his head. "Do you know, all this time, he's never told me that somber tale. No matter how many times I've asked to know what happened to my mother, he's refused to speak of her. All I knew was that the laird's first son was killed and it was her fault. When I was younger, I didn't know why he hated me so much. But not knowing the reason didn't keep it from hurting. Later, I realized he couldn't love me because I wasn't the son he wanted."

Kieran walked in a small circle before coming back to continue on.

"And now, I'm not sure if I should even call him *father*. From what he said, we can't be positive I'm his son at all. I have no mark to prove who I am." Kieran nodded toward the man's arm.

Brody pointed between them.

"We have similarities to our father. I do not doubt you are my brother."

Kieran let out a breath. At least he wasn't completely alone in the world. It seemed strange that Brody had been the one stolen away and left to wander in a strange land, yet Kieran had felt like the one who didn't belong all this time.

"I think maybe your life was not so easy," Brody said, wincing.

Kieran shrugged. "It's the only life I know. There were people who cared about me." Teague and Ella.

"But not our father." It wasn't a question.

Kieran tossed another stone into the water and watched as the ripples stretched out across the surface.

"I can't imagine having to look into the face of the person you hated. The person who caused you so much pain, day after day," Kieran said.

"But you were *not* the person that caused that pain.

The auld laird loved me like his own children by blood. Our father should have been able to see you were an innocent child. He should have loved you."

Kieran expected to feel jealous of his brother for the life he'd been given. He had all the people here who treated him as family, and yet he was also loved instantly by their father as well. But Brody wasn't the reason Rolfe hated Kieran. He wasn't to blame for being born of love, any more than Kieran was to blame for being born of manipulation and misery.

"I know I have no right to ask you for anything, but I will need your help learning my role as heir. I never imagined I would one day be in charge of a clan. I fear there is much to learn."

"Fortunately, father is hale and hearty. You will have time to learn the extent of your duties. I would be happy to help, but I fear I was never . . . suitable. You won't want my assistance if you wish to succeed."

"I'm sure that's not—"

They were interrupted when their father stepped out of the woods.

They both fell quiet. Kieran felt his shoulders sag with the weight of the man's disapproval. The same weight he'd carried as long as he could remember.

"If you don't mind, I'd like to speak to my son," he

said.

Kieran nodded and turned to leave, but Brody had also turned away.

"Kieran, please stay," the laird said.

Confusion pulled at Kieran's brows as he turned to stand before his father. Why would his father send Brody away?

"Is there something wrong?" Kieran asked when his father stood in stillness for a full minute. Kieran expected his father would only want to speak to him alone because Kieran had displeased him in some way. Probably the way he'd nearly run from the table.

No doubt, his abrupt exit had embarrassed his father. As was normal, Kieran braced himself to hear how he was, yet again, a disappointment. He should have had a bit more wine. He was not as numb as he would have liked for this conversation.

"Yes," his father finally said. "I'm afraid there is something very wrong."

Kieran stood straighter, awaiting his father's criticism, as always. As a man, he was better able to let it wash over him. But he was already raw and bleeding from the events of the day.

"*I* have been wrong for so many years. It is strange that I only just realized it today." His father shook his head as if baffled. Kieran felt just as confused.

"I'm afraid I don't understand," Kieran admitted.

"Of course, you don't. I don't know that I do myself."

Kieran swallowed. Unsure what to say, he said nothing and waited.

"I heard part of your conversation with Brody. He asked for your help, and you don't feel you are capable of providing proper guidance. Because I have found you lacking in everything you do. Christ, lad. Why haven't ye drawn a blade across my throat by now?"

Rolfe chuckled darkly while Kieran stared wide-eyed at this strange man who had taken over his father's body.

"I would never . . ."

"I know you are loyal to me, Kieran, despite the fact I've given you no reason to be."

"You are my—"

"Laird? Father? They are naught but words until someone acts as such, and I have not been a good father to you. And yet despite my shortcomings, you have become a fine man."

Kieran looked away, unsure how to respond to praise from a man who had never offered it before. He was unsettled, as if he had woken and found the sky green and the grass blue.

"I was a fool," Rolfe continued. "I focused everything I was on missing what I had lost. It left me unable to see what I did have. I had you."

"Yes, but you were not sure I was truly your son. It's understandable you—"

"No, Kieran. You were a babe. Even if I doubted your blood, you were still my son. The bloody Campbells treated Brody—a stranger—better than I treated my own child. I am ashamed. For all I have missed Muriel, she would be appalled for the way I treated an innocent boy."

Kieran didn't know what to say. He searched desperately for words but found none existed for this situation. He might have thought it a dream, but he had never imagined such a thing even in sleep.

"I am sorry for it, Kieran. It was only as I thought of all the time I'd lost with Brody that I realized I had lost as much time with you, and there was no reason for me to have missed out on being your father. I would like to do better. If you will allow me another chance."

Kieran nodded and managed to get enough words out to answer.

"Yes. Of course."

"Good. Then let us start this minute. You spoke to your brother about a woman you are in love with. Tell me."

Kieran blinked. It seemed like years since he'd mentioned Ella.

"It's Ellisay."

"Teague's daughter? The two of you have been friends since you were babes. And you love her?"

"Yes. Though I didn't realize it until recently."

His father's brows came together. "I didn't know. Why did you not want to marry her?"

"I—I knew I would have to marry for an alliance. It was my duty to marry who you chose for me. I knew you wouldn't approve."

Rolfe nodded.

"I am a fraud. I speak of loving Muriel, and yet I forced you to marry someone you didn't love. Do you know I was betrothed to marry another when I met her and begged my father to allow it? He paid a hefty price to get us out of the contract. And even after that, I forced you to turn your back on the very thing I cherished all my days. I want you to be with the woman who fills your days with happiness."

Kieran took a step closer to look his father in the eye. To find out this was but a cruel jest after he'd allowed himself to hope would bring him to his knees.

"You would give your permission for me to marry Ella?"

"Yes. Obviously, you also need to get permission from Teague, as he's her father, but I will bless the marriage so long as he does."

It was all Kieran could do to stay in place. He so much

wanted to run from this spot and find the war chief to shake the blessing from him as well. And then Kieran would jump on his horse and ride for Girnigoe immediately.

Rolfe smiled. Something he'd never done with such happiness in Kieran's direction before.

"You want to go to her now?"

"Yes. I never thought it possible. I can hardly stay still." Kieran laughed in his father's presence for the first time in many years. It felt strange not to worry or expect a rebuke.

Rolfe clapped him on the shoulder and nodded toward the path they'd used to get to the loch.

"Then let us go and speak to Teague, and you will leave at dawn. The sooner to see your love."

*

Ella lay in her aunt's cottage, looking up at the thatched roof above her, and wondered how her life had changed so quickly. It did not seem so long ago she'd been looking up at the thatching of the roof in the cottage she'd shared with her father after waking from heated dreams about Kieran.

Even more recently, she had lain in the hayloft looking up at the thatched roof of the stables after having just made love to Kieran.

And now she was here at Kildary, betrothed to a man who was kind and witty and handsome. But she did not love him.

She would *come* to love him. She wouldn't stop trying until her heart gave up and ceded to her wishes.

"I fear if you flop around any more, you'll throw yourself from the bed," Jenny warned.

"Sorry, auntie."

"You've been quiet since we returned from the castle."

"Aye. I have much to think about."

"I noticed you and Arran went up to the battlements. Did he steal a kiss?"

"Auntie! Ye shouldn't ask such a thing. You should be struck horrified by the thought of a man kissing me."

"Oh, posh. I want ye to be happy. Not much to be happy about if a handsome man doesn't steal a kiss once in a while."

"Well, he didn't steal a kiss. I gave it to him."

"Even better. What else did you give him?"

Ella knew her aunt wished for some juicy scandal. Instead, Ella shocked her by telling her the truth.

"I gave him my hand in marriage."

"What?" The next few moments were filled with sounds of Jenny getting out of her bed across the cottage and scrambling to light a candle. "Get out of your bed and tell me the rest while I pour us a bit of wine. Ye weren't sleeping anyway."

Ella agreed she wouldn't find any sleep staring up at the roof thatch and thinking about all the ways her life was changing.

"Are you happy he asked so quickly?"

"Aye. I'm happy."

Jenny held the candle closer and frowned.

"Ye don't look happy."

"I will be happy. It's just at the moment, I feel like I've been caught in a wave and no matter how much I try to stand, I get knocked down at the same time the sand beneath my feet shifts so I canna get my footing."

"Do you mean it in a good way or a bad way?"

"When is such a thing ever good? Do you even know what it's like to have sand wedged in all your delicate places, auntie?"

Jenny chuckled and held out a cup of wine to her. Ella took it, hoping it would help her sleep. She drank it down in a few gulps. Jenny poured her some more.

"I am certain you did not expect him to ask so soon. But it is a good thing to know he could not wait another minute. Yes?"

"Yes."

Jenny drank her wine in silence, which was unlike her.

Unable to take another moment of quiet, Ella opened her mouth and all sorts of things came out.

She told her aunt everything. Even how she'd given herself to Kieran. How wonderful it was. The pain in saying goodbye when she knew she loved him.

After all the ranting, Ella was surprised by Jenny's simple response.

"Damn you, Rolfe Sinclair."

Ella didn't argue, for Rolfe Sinclair was the source of all her problems, but it was strange that Jenny held such disregard for someone she didn't know.

"I told ye about my problems with Roger and my sisters, but I haven't told you of my one true love. The man I was to marry who fell in love with another and left me."

Ella gasped and shook her head. "Who?"

"Who is no matter, the reason I am bringing it up is that life is like that wave you mentioned. Sometimes it casts you up on jagged rocks strife with pain, while other times you land safely on soft sand with the sun warming your face. But regardless of what comes at you, you must always stand back up, child."

Ella nodded.

"Aye, auntie. I'm ready to stand up again."

Chapter Twenty-Four

"She did *what?*" Kieran croaked after hearing Teague explain that Ella had left Girnigoe the same day they had left to go to Kildary in the hope of marrying Arran Sutherland.

Kieran had seen resolve in Ella's eyes when they'd said their goodbyes. He'd known they would never spend time together again as they had. He'd imagined she would simply avoid the castle. Assumed she would keep to the village, where she and her father lived. He'd wanted her to find love and marry and have a happy life, but not the very day he'd left.

But, of course, he realized that was a selfish thing for him to want. If she'd been hurting, it made sense to do something to make the hurting stop. Even if that something was to marry.

"I must leave right away," Kieran said, knowing he could still be too late.

"You'll not do her any good if you kill yourself riding in the dark. Dawn is only a few hours away, and you'll be able to ride faster in the light," his brother said.

"Aye. Get some rest and wait until morning. You'll need your strength," his father added. It still baffled Kieran that his father was smiling at him. Concerned for his happiness. Kieran almost expected to wake up and find this were all a dream.

But if Ella married Arran, it would surely turn into a nightmare.

He turned back to Teague.

"You have not yet given your blessing. I may fail in my task to get to her in time, but if I succeed, do I have your permission to wed her?"

Teague smiled and pulled him into a hug, slapping him on the back.

"Aye. The two of ye have had a happy life thus far, so it goes that you would have a happy future as well." Teague's smile slipped. "I hope you won't be too late."

Kieran had agreed he needed rest after the stress of the past days, but he found it near to impossible to sleep as he lay in a bed in the Campbell keep while counting down the minutes until the dawn.

Giving up, he went down and found the kitchens, asking one of the maids for some food he could take with him on his journey. He went to the stable to fetch and tack his horse. When the cook brought him a bundle of bannocks, cheese, and fruit, he thanked her and packed it away for later.

His stomach was much too twisted to eat now.

He wasn't expecting his father to be waiting in the bailey to see him off.

"I knew you would be off with the sun and wanted to wish you safe travels."

"Thank ye, father. I only hope I am not too late."

Rolfe patted Ridire. "I hope to see you at home with your love by your side. We will plan a fine wedding."

"I want it like I've never wanted anything else."

With that, they exchanged a nod and Kieran rode out through the gate.

"Come on, Ridire. We must get there before it's too late."

*

"Arran is a good man," Ella said as she paced her aunt's cottage.

"So you've said, numerous times." Jenny frowned at the needle grasped in her fingers.

"You don't think he is a good man?" Ella asked, coming to stop in front of her aunt. Ever since Arran had proposed, she'd worried she'd done the right thing by agreeing.

Then, when he'd suggested marrying right away, she'd felt as if she had been pulled along in his excitement and had agreed to that too. And why wouldn't she want to marry straightaway?

What good would come of waiting? She was committed to this path. Might as well start walking it.

But now, having slept on it, doubts crept in.

"I do think he is a fine man, I'm just not sure why you feel the need to mention it yet again."

"He is handsome," Ella went on, now that her aunt had agreed to him being a good, fine man.

"Aye."

"A fierce fighter, I'm sure." Though she'd not had the opportunity to see him in action.

"Being the war chief would guarantee such," Jenny reasoned.

Ella nodded. It was true enough. Her Uncle William wouldn't have given him such a responsibility if he weren't up for the task.

"He has a quick wit."

"Humor will get you through many of the storms life brings."

Storms. She felt as if she were already caught up in such a storm.

"I believe he will be faithful," Ella continued.

"As a good man would do."

"Yes. He is a good man."

Jenny let out a sigh and tilted her head.

"You would tell me if I'm readying this gown for nothing."

"Aye. It is not for nothing. In fact, I wish it was ready right now so I might go find him and have it done right away. Maybe this evening after the meal? Today would be a good day. Better, I think, than tomorrow, as planned."

"I will sew faster if you wish."

"I don't think I even need a fancy gown to marry. I could just marry like this." She gestured to herself.

"In breeches, ye mean?" Jenny frowned.

Ella had thought a long ride that morning might settle her nerves, but it hadn't worked.

"Aye. Shouldn't the man I marry love me in breeches as well as a gown?"

"Did Arran say he loved ye?" Jenny settled her gaze on Ella.

"Well, nay. It is too soon for such emotions, and we have not spent so much time together."

Not very much time at all. But then Kieran was to marry a woman he'd never met and didn't know if he would even like, so did one need so much time to decide? If one was sure they were willing to do their best to make it a good match, what else was there to decide?

"Do you think you should spend more time with him before ye marry to make sure this is the right thing?" Jenny asked.

"Nay. I think we should get it done so we might move forward. It would be easier to get to know each other after we're married so we can spend all our time together."

"Could you sit down? All your pacing is making me dizzy and stirring up dust."

"Did you not marry because you loved Roger? The man that seduced you as well as your sisters?"

"Nay, once I learned of his true nature, I was able to see he wasn't worth my heart."

"You said there was another. Someone else who stole your heart."

"Aye, but I don't want to speak of it. Nothing comes of wishing for things."

"Nothing comes from living for something you can't have. That is why I am going to live for the thing I *can* have.

And Arran is the thing—the person, rather—I can have."

"We are not so easily traded out for another, lass."

"I know. That is why I am glad that Arran is a—"

"A good man," Jenny interrupted, already knowing what Ella was going to say.

"Aye. Sew faster, auntie. I wish to marry today." Ella gave her aunt a squeeze.

*

Kieran stopped only to water his horse and take a bite to eat. The closer he got to Kildary, the more he felt he was going to be too late.

He had known Ella his whole life, so he knew well enough the way she jumped right into something as soon as her mind was made up.

How many times had she asked him why they needed to wait once they had decided to do something? Despite her reckless nature, she rarely had any regrets.

Kieran, on the other hand, was the opposite. He was too cautious. He waited too long to act, thinking through any possible reason he should not proceed.

The two of them were perfectly suited in this way. She pulling him into living, while he gave the pause needed to ensure their plan was sound. Together they were balanced.

In this decision, to ride off and hopefully stop her from marrying another, Kieran suffered no delays or doubts. He only prayed he would make it in time.

She would not have considered the possibility that he would come for her. That he would be free to marry her. Even if the Campbells had not agreed to give up Isla to be his bride, another bride would have been selected for the heir of the Sinclairs, and that bride never would have been her.

She couldn't know how much had happened in the last few days. That everything had changed and he was free to marry her.

He couldn't wait to see the shock on her face when he told her the tale. He doubted she would believe him when he told her how his father had apologized and even hugged him. Or that the laird himself had seen Kieran off to go find Ella so they could marry.

It was pouring rain as Kieran crested the final hill that allowed his view of Balnagown Castle. The Ross keep sat on a rocky hill, its gray stone the same color of the steely sky above. The rain stung Kieran's face as he nudged Ridire a little faster.

Despite the glum appearance, Kieran's heart lifted.

He was almost there.

"Please don't let me be too late."

*

Ella knocked on the heavy wooden door and grew nervous as she heard footfalls approach.

Arran opened the door and blinked for a moment in what she guessed was confusion before he frowned and opened the door wider.

"Ella? What has happened? You're soaked through. Come sit by the fire. We must warm you up."

In truth, she was not cold, or at least she had not noticed. But her teeth were near to chattering.

Arran sat her in a large chair before the flames and grabbed a fur from his bed to drape around her.

She had been right all along. Arran was a good man. He just wasn't going to be the man for her.

As she'd continued in her pacing and talking with Aunt Jenny, she'd realized the answer to the question she had refused to ask herself.

Was this fair to Arran?

She had wanted to marry so she would not have to suffer alone with the loss of Kieran. She had been content to marry a good man despite not loving him. She had thought she could be happy enough with him.

But what of him? What was he getting out of this?

"You are not dressed," he pointed out, then smiled.

"Unless you plan to marry me in breeches. I would not mind, for you are quite fetching in them. But it might cause talk in the hall." He winked at her, and she felt her bottom lip tremble.

"I am sorry, Arran." She broke into tears, causing Arran to look stricken with concern for her. She didn't deserve his goodness.

"I'm sure you've nothing to be sorry for, Ella. Everything will be fine when we marry. I'll make sure you never have cause for tears."

She shook her head. He could not make such promises.

Life wasn't to be lived without tears. Marriage didn't bring a guarantee that everything would be perfect from the moment the vows were spoken. It was a pledge that whatever brought tears would never be faced alone.

"Why do you want to marry me?" she managed to ask.

He cleared his throat before answering, "There are so many reasons they are too great to think of just one."

"Then tell me two or maybe three," she said.

"Oh. Well . . . you are clever and witty. I enjoy conversing with you."

She nodded.

"You are lovely. Any man would be proud to call you his wife."

So far, she couldn't find fault with his reasons, but then he seemed to stall. He looked into the fire as if mesmerized by the flames.

"I believe I shall need to hear a third thing," she prompted. If the third thing convinced her he was happy, she would go back to Jenny's cottage and change into her wedding gown right away.

Arran shook his head. "I'm afraid the third reason might well be the true reason, and I don't wish to say it."

She stood and placed her hand on his arm.

"We should be able to tell each other anything, even if it is difficult, should we not?"

He nodded and let out a sigh.

"I came to Kildary to get away from my own clan. I had been in love with a girl there, and she married another. Here at Balnagown, I hoped to end my pain in battle. I gave my sword to the Ross laird and ran into the fray of battle with no care of walking back out. But I did. Over and over, I survived. And your uncle thought me so brave he gave me the honor of being his war chief. And little by little, I started to care again that I walked off the battlefield. But . . ."

"The pain didn't go away? You thought marrying someone you cared for would help?"

He looked at her as if he thought her a witch for reading his mind. Then he nodded.

"I take it you are in a similar situation? You have given your heart to another and hoped to scrape up enough happiness in a marriage with someone whom you saw only as a friend?"

She nodded again.

"Kieran?" he guessed.

She wiped at her tears and nodded.

"It was foolish to lose my heart to him, for he is being married to another. And even if the contract falls through, he would never be mine. Why can we not cling to what we *can* have rather than suffer the rest of our lives for what we cannot?"

He slumped into the chair next to her.

"I am ashamed," he said. "I had hoped you would be enough to heal my heart. But that is not fair to you. To ask you to take on such a burden."

"And to know we would be destined to fail?"

He nodded and then let out a painful laugh.

"Do ye think this is what happens with all marriages? Is it just one long line of people marrying people they can have to ease the suffering? On and on."

"I am beginning to wonder," she said, and his lips pulled up just a hint on one side.

"It seemed like it might work, didn't it?" he asked. For the first time, she saw the pain in his eyes. She imagined it had been there all that time if she had only looked.

"Aye. I so badly wish it would work." She watched the flames for a minute or two before speaking again. "Perhaps if we were to give ourselves time to heal from our pain and then try again with a different purpose?"

He nodded. "Aye. That sounds quite reasonable."

"And how long do you think it will take? To heal, I mean?"

He shook his head. "I do not know, but I am in my second year of trying to mend my broken heart. I really thought I was ready."

Good God, if she would bear this pain for two years, she didn't think she would survive it. Then she thought of Jenny and how long she had been trying to heal.

"I can say," he went on with a heartier smile, "it has begun to get easier. I don't recommend drinking or fighting. It only adds to your misery. But talking with a friend helps. So I thank you, Ella. For being such a friend to me."

She nodded. "Thank you, Arran."

She left his room feeling she had done the right thing, but she was no closer to happiness for it.

.

Chapter Twenty-Five

Jenny was waiting with a warm blanket and a cup of hot tea.

"Ye called it off?"

"Aye. It wasn't fair to either of us," Ella explained.

"What will you do?"

It was a good question. For once, Ella was not sure of her next step. Kieran always teased her about making such quick decisions and acting on them without thought. It was true enough she didn't often find herself in a situation where she couldn't determine the next step.

But for maybe the first time, she faltered. She'd

thought marrying Arran would be the next step, but with that option removed, she was lost.

"I will stay here with you, auntie."

Jenny frowned.

"You are always welcome in my home, but there is danger in hiding away from the struggles of life, Ella."

"I don't wish to hide away all my life. Just until it doesn't hurt quite so bad."

Jenny shook her head.

"Ye should be prepared, lass. It may always hurt."

She was about to ask her aunt what pained her when someone banged on the door.

Ella got up to answer it. Before she got there, another round of knocking shook the heavy wood.

Opening it, she stared at the man towering above her. Rain streamed over his black hair, dripping from the tips onto his shoulders. He blinked his green eyes at her.

"Please tell me you aren't wed," Kieran said as a greeting.

She might have lectured him, but she had never seen him so serious.

"Nay. I'm not."

"Good, then." He ducked inside and pulled her into his arms to kiss her. It was not just a little peck. Nay, it was a claiming of her lips and soul. She tasted his frantic worry, relief, and . . . joy.

When he set her down, he asked, "Will ye marry *me*, Ella?"

"I—I don't understand." He was supposed to be married already. "Did the Campbells not turn over your bride? You'll surely be contracted with another."

"Nay. The Sinclair heir has married Isla as planned."

She blinked and tilted her head to the side.

"Then why are you here kissing me?"

"It turns out, I am not the Sinclair heir. There is much that has happened. The most important part is I am free and have permission from both your father and mine to marry you, Ella. So long as you say yes."

"Hold," Jenny said as she came closer. "I was given the duty of approving a match for my niece. You'll need my blessing as well."

Kieran smiled before walking to stand before Aunt Jenny. He bowed and took both her hands in his.

"Will ye please give me your blessing to wed your niece? She is the only person I want to spend my life with, to have a family with, and to grow old with. I beg of ye."

Jenny pulled her hand away and gave him a shove.

"Aye. I give my blessing, so long as ye stop dripping all over my floor."

They all laughed at that.

Kieran turned to Ella again.

"Will ye—"

Her answer was to tackle him and kiss him while muttering, "Aye," over and over.

*

Kieran told Ella and Jenny the whole story as they rode for home.

"Your brother lives? All this time?" Ella asked for the third time.

"Aye. And he's quite nice. So is his Isla, so long as I'm not meant to marry her." He winked at his newly betrothed.

"And what of your father? Is he happy?" Jenny was the one to ask. She was traveling with them so she could see Ella married. But something in her question surprised Kieran.

"You know my father?"

"Aye. He fostered with my father. How do ye think he and Teague became such friends?" She waved a hand. "It is all in the past. He returned home and met Muriel, and any plans he had made prior were turned to ash."

He and Ella shared a look, both noticing the sadness in Jenny's words.

"What plans, auntie?"

"It doesn't matter."

"It may not matter, but I'd still like to know," Ella pushed as only she could. Kieran couldn't wait for them to be married, but they had both decided they wished to be married on the beach at Caithness, as it was most likely the place where they grew to love one another.

"Rolfe and I were betrothed to marry," Jenny said matter-of-factly.

Kieran reined his horse to a stop and found Ella doing the same, turning to look at her aunt.

"You were to marry the Sinclair laird?"

"Aye. As I said, it was long ago. I fell in love with him when he was but a lanky boy sparring with Teague and William. He asked me to marry him before he left, and I said yes. But then he met Muriel when he returned home. He wrote to tell me his heart was otherwise engaged and we were not to be."

Kieran hoped Ella would know what to say, for he did not. He shouldn't have doubted.

"Are you certain you wish to return to Caithness now? Will it be too painful for you? I know you have never moved on from this, and I don't wish for my wedding to cause you any pain."

"I'm ready to face it," she said. "Besides, I'll not miss getting to watch you marry your best friend."

"If you need to leave, you'll let me know, and I'll see you escorted home right away," Kieran promised.

As someone who had also been harmed by Rolfe Sinclair, Kieran would protect Jenny as much as was possible.

"Thank ye, Kieran. But it is time. If nothing else, I will tell him how very angry I am with him, and if he is honorable enough to apologize, I will forgive him. I believe I need to forgive him. And then mayhap I can finally let go of my hurt and find happiness. Seeing Ella following in my path made me see it is no way to live. I didn't want it for her, and now I see I don't want it for myself either."

Kieran thought he understood. His father had expressed his regrets for how he'd treated Kieran, and it had lifted a weight from his shoulders. He would hope the same for Ella's aunt.

It was Brody who rode out to meet them when they were close enough to Castle Girnigoe to alert the guards.

"Ella, Jenny, may I introduce ye to my brother, Br— Aiden."

Brody laughed. "It is fine. I am learning to answer to both names."

Jenny stared and then said, "My, but ye look exactly like your father at that age."

"That is not the first time I have heard so. In fact, it's not the first time today," Brody joked. "But surely, the first time today by one as lovely as ye, Lady Jenny."

Brody turned to Ella. "I am hopeful you are here because you plan to become my sister?"

"Aye."

"Good. That means he arrived in time to snatch you up for himself."

They laughed and turned for the castle.

The laird was waiting for them when they rode into the bailey. It was still a surprise to see the man smiling. But he was fairly beaming when they dismounted.

Isla was there as well, and while his sister-in-law was bonny, Kieran was beyond glad he didn't have to marry her. He smiled at his betrothed, happier than he could ever remember being.

Helping Ella down, he noticed his father stepped closer to help Jenny from her horse. Kieran couldn't help but notice the way Ella's aunt smiled at his father in a rather dazed way.

"Jenny, it's been some time," Kieran's father said.

"Aye. Ye seem happy," she replied.

"There is much to be happy for. Both of my sons have returned to the castle with their women. And a lovely guest as well. We have a great deal of celebrating to do."

Kieran and Ella shared a look, and, as was common for them, he understood what she was thinking, or rather what she was baffled about. It seemed his father and her aunt were flirting with one another, and Rolfe had only barely looked away from Jenny since she'd arrived in the bailey.

Mayhap there was some more happiness to be had in the Sinclair keep today.

Glancing over to his lost brother, Brody smiled with his wife beside him. It was strange to think of how many times he had cursed his faceless brother for leaving him with a grief-stricken father and shoes too big for Kieran to ever fill.

But they were a family now. Despite how or where they'd been raised, this would be their home and their children's home.

When Teague came up to claim his sister in a hug, Rolfe turned to Kieran to ask, "When do ye plan to marry?"

"Today," Ella answered quickly, then pressed her lips together as if realizing the question hadn't been directed to her.

Kieran laughed at her excitement and nodded.

"Aye. I believe today will be long enough for us to wait. I would have wed her at the Ross keep, but all of our family is here now."

Teague pulled Ella close and whispered, "I'm so glad ye didn't already marry the Sutherland."

"I couldn't. I didn't love him."

"And ye love *him*?" Teague nodded in Kieran's direction. "Even after he made ye sick and broke your hand when ye were a lass?"

"Da, we were practically bairns, and he didn't do it on purpose."

"Aye. I did give him my blessing already, so I guess I can't go back on it."

"Would you wish to?" she asked, tilting her head.

"Nay. No one has ever made you as happy as this lad. And I expect him to continue doing so." This was said in Kieran's direction, and he nodded as Ella stepped close enough for him to tuck her against his side, where she fit perfectly.

Mayhap because she had always belonged there.

And always would.

Epilogue

Kieran sat in the hall next to his father. His brother was also seated at the high table as they listened to clan disputes together. Brody had taken his place at the right hand of the Sinclair laird.

But despite having an older brother to divide Rolfe's attentions, Kieran had never felt closer to his father. The man still offered apologies at times for the lack of love in Kieran's early years.

Kieran often told him the past was in the past. Besides, Kieran was not in short supply of love and family any longer.

"I tell ye, laird, the man has switched my cow," Innes

complained while Archie rolled his eyes.

"'Tis the same cow ye've always had. You're losing your mind ye auld fool."

The laird leaned toward Kieran.

"What do ye think we should do about this?" he asked. "And before ye answer, know that if they come in here again with more complaints of cattle switching, I may very well pull my dirk. I'll soon have grandchildren to sit on my knees, and I'll not want my time wasted with this prattle."

Rolfe Sinclair was in constant excitement for the arrival of his grandchildren. Ella and Isla had become fast friends, more sisters than even Kieran and Brody had become brothers. It was a great surprise when they'd shared with each other they were increasing to find the other was as well. And the laird couldn't have been more pleased.

Kieran laughed and leaned closer to give his opinion on the cow switching while recalling how much had changed since the last time Innes and Archibald had visited the hall.

At the time, he'd thought of Ella as only a friend. While she was still his very best friend, she was so much more. And soon their relationship would change again when she became the mother of his child.

"I think we trade Innes his cow for one of ours that we know gives milk so the man can stop his fussing. The extra milk might put some coin in his pocket while helping his neighbors as well."

"Aye. I think it worth the loss of one cow just to shut the man up."

Brody leaned over to add his advice. "Might we make sure the cow we give him looks nothing like Archibald's cow so he canna complain again?"

Both Rolfe and Kiernan nodded in agreement.

Rolfe opened his mouth to give his ruling but paused and smiled when Jenny walked into the room. She cast him a saucy look before heading toward the kitchen.

Kieran and Brody exchanged a smile behind their father's back. Rolfe and Jenny had been spending a good bit of time together, and Brody had told Kieran two mornings past he had seen Jenny sneaking out of their father's bedchamber just before dawn.

"Ye should marry her, father," Kieran said.

"I have asked three times already. She said I made her wait all these years. She is going to make me wait a bit." While he seemed piqued, he smiled.

"I believe our father has met his match," Brody laughed.

"All the more reason for us to get this cattle business cleared up so I might attempt to woo her into agreeing today," Rolfe said.

Clearing his throat, the laird prepared to speak again

when he was interrupted by a maid who came rushing down the stairs and into the room.

"It's time! The babe is coming."

"Which one?" Kieran asked at the same time his brother said, "Who's babe is coming?"

The maid looked between Kieran and Brody before answering. "Both!"

*

Ella had been having a bit of pain since she woke that morning, but now as afternoon was upon them, the pain had grown more intense.

"Are you well, sister?" Isla asked. "You look rather pale."

After all these months, it still seemed odd to have someone call her *sister*. But despite the strangeness, the two women had become like sisters to each other.

From the moment they realized they were both carrying Sinclair babes, they were a constant support for all the struggles that came with increasing.

"I've had a bit of pain," Ella admitted.

Isla nodded. "I thought as much. Are the pains growing closer together?"

Ella nodded. "They have, but up until just now, the

pain was not so great. Now, the little devil seems to be set on getting my attention."

Isla smiled as she affectionately rubbed her own belly.

Their men had made a joke out of declaring whose babe would come sooner. Ella opened her mouth to tell Isla she and Kieran would surely have the first babe, when another pain came right on top of the first, this one with more force than the first.

Letting out a moan of pain, Isla came closer and Ella saw her reach for her before the woman pulled her hands back with a startled, "Oh."

"What is it?" Ella asked, but the soft splash on the stones between Isla's feet answered her question.

They shared a look and then a smile before they both shouted for the maid that was always close by.

Everything happened in a flurry. The healer was brought to Isla's room first and then next door to check on Ella. Kieran nearly pushed the woman out of his way, the faster to get to her side.

"Ella, are you well?"

"Nay, I've your giant babe inside me who wants to be set free."

Kieran smiled and kissed her forehead, which had broken out in a sweat.

"Ye are fierce, Ellie. I know this will be easy work for

someone as strong as ye."

"If you're saying so because you want me to push our child out before Isla, you can just keep it to yourself. I know we made jests about it, but I can only care about what is happening in this room."

Kieran shook his head. "I don't mind if our niece or nephew is born before our son or daughter. So long as everyone is hale and hearty at the end." He kissed the back of her hand and then pressed his lips together.

She knew him well enough to know he was trying not to say something.

"What is it?" she asked, knowing if he asked her to hurry she would cross her legs and hold it until she heard a child's cry from the room next door.

"I want to stay with ye. Brody and I spoke a few days ago about wanting to be with our wives while they went through this battle. Please don't cast me out to worry in the corridor. To wear down the stones with my pacing. I will do whatever ye ask, but please. Let me stay here with ye."

She might have answered, but another pain was upon her. She grasped her husband's large hand and squeezed tight until the pain subsided. She looked at him to see if he'd gone pale or planned to swoon, but he nodded at her.

"I am here, wife. Just as I've been all our lives. Whatever you need, you have only to ask and I'll see it done."

"Isla said we would be there for each other no matter who went first. We weren't expecting this. So I would welcome your help," she said. After all, it was the two of the them in all things.

Jenny came into Ella's room with a big grin. She looked over at Kieran, who made no effort to even pretend he was leaving. Jenny just shook her head and came to Ella's other side, taking her hand.

"Isla is as far along as ye. I may be needed to deliver your babe as we've only the one healer."

Ella nodded.

True to his word, Kieran did his duty, wiping her brow with cool water and allowing her to squeeze his hand and curse at him as she labored. But eventually, hours later, while it was still dark outside, their child was born.

In the bits of silence between their son's cries, Ella heard another babe just as displeased in the room next to her.

Jenny handed their babe to Kieran, who smiled down at the bundle with glistening eyes.

"Oh, Ella, you did so well," he said as he settled the babe in her arms. Blue eyes looked up at her as she ran a hand over the white fuzz atop his head.

"If I didna know better, I'd swear we have the babe that belongs next door."

They shared a laugh as Ella stared at her child.

A soft knock sounded at the door, and Kieran went to open it only a crack so no one could see in.

"We've a son," she heard Brody say.

"Aye. We've a son as well. How is Isla?"

"She is well. Our women are fierce, brother."

"Aye, they are," Kieran agreed.

"I must get back to my family," Brody said before the door closed again, and Kieran returned to sit on the side of her bed.

"I can't believe how happy I am, Ella," Kieran said as he smiled in awe at their child. When he looked up at her, she saw the way his green eyes glistened with tears and the bright smile pulling up the lips she kissed each night before sleep.

"I believe it was time for all of us to have some happiness, don't you?" she asked.

He leaned over to kiss her as he nodded.

"Aye. I believe it is."

The end.

Author's Note

Thank you for reading The Highland Heir! If you've read my Clan MacKinlay Series, keep reading. If not… spoilers ahead.

You may have recognized some parts of this story reminded you of a similar situation at the end of Her Forbidden Highlander Husband. When that series had ended, I found myself thinking often about the character, David, from that book and how things would have been for him.

As I considered his story, his character morphed into Kieran, and since he was his own person, and the outcome was somewhat different, I decided to expand it into its own book.

Thank you for allowing me the freedom to explore that story.

As always… I write historical romance, not history books. I do my best to strive for accuracy, but at times I cling to the fiction element for the benefit of the story. Please forgive any errors on mistakes on my part.

Also from Allison B. Hanson...

Clan MacKinlay Series

Her Accidental Highlander Husband

Her Reluctant Highlander Husband

Her Forbidden Highlander Husband

Coming in 2024...

Clan MacPherson Series

His Secret Highland Bride

His Forgotten Highland Bride

His Captivating Highland Bride

Scots and Scoundrels Series

Winning Her Duke

Discovering Her Earl

Seducing Her Viscount

Learn about other books available on my website

www.allisonbhanson.com

About the Author

One very early morning, Allison B. Hanson woke up with a conversation going on in her head. It wasn't so much a dream as being forced awake by her imagination. Unable to go back to sleep, she gave in, went to the computer, and began writing. Years later it still hasn't stopped.

Allison's historical romances are filled with kilted heroes of the cinnamon roll variety.

She lives near Hershey, Pennsylvania, and enjoys candy immensely, as well as long motorcycle rides, running and reading.

Printed in Great Britain
by Amazon

29017544R00169